W9-DBQ-203

Buckskin Man

Buckskin Man

TOM W. BLACKBURN

Sagebrush
Large Print Westerns

Library of Congress Cataloging in Publication Data

Blackburn, Thomas Wakefield.
  Buckskin man / Tom W. Blackburn.
    p.   cm.
  ISBN 1-57490-180-X (lg. print : alk. paper)
  1. Large type books. I. Title.
  [PS3552.L3422B83   1999]
  813'.54–dc21   98-50924
                                                             CIP

Cataloguing in Publication Data is available from
the British Library and the National Library of Australia.

Sagebrush Large Print Westerns are published in the United
States and Canada by Thomas T. Beeler, Publisher, Box 659,
Hampton Falls, New Hampshire 03844-0659. ISBN 1-57490-180-X

Published in the United Kingdom, Eire, and the Republic of South
Africa by Isis Publishing Ltd, 7 Centremead, Osney Mead, Oxford
OX2 0ES England. ISBN 0-7531-6008-0

Published in Australia and New Zealand by Australian Large Print
Audio & Video Pty Ltd, 17 Mohr Street, Tullamarine, Victoria, 3043,
Australia. ISBN 1-86442-268-8

Manufactured in the United States of America by BookCrafters, Inc.

Buckskin Man

CHAPTER 1

THE PARROQUIA BELLS

WAR WAS INEVITABLE. ALL WARS WERE INEVITABLE. Somebody had something and somebody else wanted it. So there was war. Or murder, or a fist fight, or name calling and libel, or a neatly turned business deal, or a swindle. All of it war, one way or another. And suddenly the somebody who had something didn't have it any more. The somebody who wanted it did. That was history.

The Mexican War had been inevitable. Fernando Portola had said that from the beginning. Portola hated *yanquis*. Not in person, perhaps, but in principle. He always said it this way. He had said it that way last night, publicly publishing his say about the war again. His authoritative old voice had rung through the room, dominating the whole party as the old man had long dominated Santa Fe. His daughter had not stopped dancing, but his two sons had nodded grim agreement with their father. For a wonder, there was argument, too. Plenty of it. Argument over nothing.

The war had come and gone. It was really no longer worth talking about. It was no longer worth argument. Probably this was why a few were bold enough or drunk enough to contradict Fernando Portola. But contradiction didn't make a difference any longer, either. The war was gone and Mexico was gone, also— from Santa Fe, at least. General Kearney was gone, on to California with the army. New fields to conquer. There were a few uniforms left, to be sure. Sterling

1

Price, with his uneasy colonelcy and a couple of hundred men to garrison all of New Mexico under her new striped flag. But they didn't count.

About all that was left was argument. That and trade. The Santa Fe trade. The river of goods and profit flowing both ways along the great trail reaching hungrily southwestward from St. Louis by way of the Missouri and St. Joe. A dollars and cents tide of fur and staple and textile and hardware. The thing the war had been about in the first place.

All that remained inevitable in Santa Fe now was that a man got drunk on Saturday night. That and Sunday's hang-over. Who gave a damn that this was the ancient city of the Holy Faith?

Jim King rolled over, then twisted abruptly back. His head refused to turn with him. It was riveted to his pillow. Leadenly riveted. It ached abominably. The sour taste of a strong man's share of last night's Taos Lightnin' was in his mouth. He shivered and opened his eyes. It was early, but the light hurt. He blinked dry lids closed, groaning.

Sunday morning. Sacred day of the pious and the godly. And him with the fur of the dog thick in his throat and the gongs of the devil clamoring in his skull. The wages of sin, no doubt. But damned if he felt guilty. Just hung over.

Jim tried rolling over again, slowly. This time he made it. The gongs of the devil within his skull altered to the bells of the Parroquia, summoning the faithful to Mass. Aside from the Spanish tongue itself, this was probably the oldest sound in Santa Fe.

Suddenly the rhythmic tolling broke into an excited clangor. Shouts echoed distantly. Jim heaved to a sitting position. At the same time he became aware of what

2

must have awakened him in the first place—the smell of smoke.

He swung his feet over the edge of the bed, stabbing them with instinctive accuracy into the moccasin boots on the floor. A man began pounding on the alley door, his voice a high-pitched Spanish alarm to anyone within. But by the time Jim reached the door the man was gone, his footfalls a diminishing clatter.

He flipped up the inner latch by its thong. The door remained fast. Someone had dropped a pin through the staple and hasp outside. It was no accident, either. Accidents didn't happen in this fashion in Santa Fe. Here alley doors in occupied buildings were fastened only from within. A natural convenience among a people who were efficient in movement if nothing else. Jim swung back into the room.

The smell of smoke was stronger. Wisps were eddying past the fit of the opposite door which led into the trade room in front. He crossed quickly to this and tried the pull. It was also fastened on the other side though Jim clearly remembered leaving it unfastened when he came back through the trade room from the plaza when he turned in.

He had carried his buckskin breeches with him from the bed to the back door. He dropped these now and dived into a corner for the rusty kindling ax he kept there. The door to the trade room splintered with his third swing and a section of the planking drove through. He reached through the hole and freed the latch on the far side and kicked the door open into an inferno.

A continuous sheet of flame spread across the front of the trade room, effectively blocking escape into the plaza. It was a rich and roaring flame, born of old floor planking, racked Missouri saddles, stands of hickory

3

tool hafting, bolted duck canvasing, and other combustible price leaders displayed near the door to catch the eye of casual retail trade. And Jim did not need his nose to realize the fire had been carefully and generously primed beforehand with lamp oil.

However, the real destruction was not in these imported goods near the front door. What really sickened him were the flames maliciously licking up oil-soaked stacks of baled furs along one side wall. Furs brought to Jim King by men of the mountain legion for shipment to the River and sale on the River markets. The season's take of a score of men who wanted no part of Duval & Co. or Saul Wetzel, and who trusted Jim King above any trader in Santa Fe because he had once been one of them. It was a staggering loss. One it was unlikely he could redeem in a dozen seasons, for it destroyed trust as well as consignment. A calculated loss, intentionally inflicted.

Some contents of the store had not yet been reached by the flames. These could be saved, but Jim made no move. A man vaulted recklessly, through the flame barricading the front door. A dark-skinned man in Sunday clothes whom Jim did not recognize. He waved the man back but the man stayed, kicking at the flames to scatter them. Others leaped through after the man, bringing slopping buckets. They wet down a passage to the plaza door.

More men poured in to attack the fire. Smoke thickened, turning Jim's scalded throat raw. These men were not fighting for him. He knew that. Among the close-packed buildings fronting this side of the plaza, threat to one was threat to all. Santa Fe had known fire before.

Turning, Jim went back through the splintered door to

4

his quarters, still carrying the ax. At the rear door he swung the ax with sudden malevolent violence. The bit sliced through stop and jamb, biting into the hasp outside. When he tugged the ax free, the door swung open.

A little knot of mestizos were gathered in the alleyway, eyes upraised. Now that the doors were open, front to back, a better draft existed and smoke boiled high above the store. The mestizos glanced curiously at Jim. One crossed himself and seemed about to speak, but Jim shouldered past him before he could. Wetzel was standing in the mouth of the alleyway, across from the rear entrance to his own store. His eyes widened at the sight of Jim and he darted out to seize his arm.

"They said you'd burned in there!" he gasped.

"Who said?"

"It's all over town."

"They didn't get me drunk enough last night. Not quite."

Wetzel still clung to his arm.

"That draft I advanced you in September, Jim. What about it, now?"

"I'll pay it when it's due."

Wetzel looked up at the black smoke boiling above the store of the King Trading Company. Jim saw the glance.

"A hell of a time to be asking about your money, Saul!" he exploded. "You'll get yours. Everybody will!"

He broke Wetzel's grip and turned out of the alleyway toward the plaza. Although the Parroquia bell was again summoning the faithful to Mass, its duty as fire alarm now done, the crowd in the plaza was unheeding. Besides, most of them were busy. A bucket line was stretched out from the front of the store and

5

there were enough hands to ensure the building itself would be saved.

Jim pushed roughly through the press to the block long veranda before the *Palacio del Gobernador*. The doors beneath this were all closed as he hurried past them. It was all right. He was not in search of the law. He had reached the far end of the veranda before he realized he had added only his boots to his sleeping attire. All that covered him from the tail of his shirt to the tops of his boots were his use-bagged underdrawers. The hell with it. Neither was this a social call. He turned the corner of the *palacio* with purposefully lengthening stride.

The only opening in the street wall of the pink adobe house on the *Calle de los Viejos* was the low archway of the main entrance, stoutly closed with a pair of planked doors. Jim knew better than to try these. Especially on a Sunday morning. Especially on this Sunday morning.

A small walk ran back along the side wall of the house. This exposure of 'dobe masonry was as devoid of windows as the front. Jim smiled grimly. They knew how to build houses in this country. Santa Fe windows turned inward, not out. Maybe because the people of the old town lacked the *yanqui* penchant for sharing intimacies with the public. A private home here was private.

At the rear of the side wall was a narrow door, set deep in the mud masonry. The latch lifted easily. Jim pushed the door open and stepped into the service portion of the house. Actually it was a separate structure, across an inner patio from the main building. A short gallery led off to the left into an open kitchen. A servant was pulling a tray of breakfast cakes out from the baking shelf let into one side of a big beehive fireplace in one corner of this room. A strange kind of servant. A big man, clumsy and unfamiliar with this sort of work. A cook with a long Green River knife at his belt. A man Jim had seen tending trade in the Duval & Co. post. One of Luis Sebastian's Jacks-of-all-trades.

The man saw Jim and pivoted, his throat swelling, but Jim plowed into him before he could shout. They went down onto the sandstone hearth. Their fall overturned a stack of cooking pots. The smallest of these, of thick cast iron and conveniently possessed of a bail, rolled beneath Jim's hand. He grabbed the bail and swung the pot. It rang dully against the cook's skull. The man stiffened in spasm and went limp. Jim swung the pot twice again to make sure.

Rising, he kicked the man ungently in the ribs, then thought of the Green River knife and his own weapon belt, back in his burning store. As he slipped the cook's blade from its sheath, he sniffed above its owner in the hope of detecting the odor of lamp oil. There was only a strong body smell. Santa Fe was not a clean town and those who worked for Duval & Co. and Luis Sebastian were not the cleanest of her citizens. Dropping the knife into the top of his right boot, Jim started out across the patio toward the main part of the house.

Luis Sebastian was at breakfast. Jim did not see him until he was nearly across the patio. There was a small table set up under a large, carefully trimmed oleander tree in a corner which the morning sun could not reach. Sebastian sat at this. He wore an immaculate, full-sleeved white broadcloth shirt, heavily starched at cuff and breast. Beneath the youthfully open collar a scarlet kerchief was crossed as though to protect the shirt from contact with the flesh of its wearer's neck. Both white and scarlet were in fine contrast to the rich golden color

7

of Sebastian's skin. In contrast, too, were his jet hair and the clean whiteness of the whites of his eyes and the brilliant whiteness of his even teeth. He wore dark, tight Spanish trousers and a pair of small, gleaming black leather slippers with no heel or heel-cup.

Jim thought grudgingly, as he had before, that Sebastian was the handsomest man he had ever seen. And he knew he was the most dangerous. He was like an exquisitely made presentation firearm. The finest of steels lay beneath the fanciful chasing and inlay, and a feather's touch upon the trigger would drop a hammer which never misfired. Sebastian's appearance and charm had brought him a constant revenue in a kind of coin for which he did not have to account to St. Louis as an agent for Duval & Co. Santa Fe might not be a clean town, but it was a beautiful one; and not merely because men seeing it for the first time were usually at the end of nine hundred and eighty-five miles of arid trail out from the River at St. Joe. The women of Santa Fe were beautiful beyond anything Missouri could boast, and many of them seemed willing to pay Sebastian his tribute. So, at least, went gossip.

Jim had been inclined to discount the talk. It was as cheap here as anywhere else. A trade and trail town was apt to abound in legends of amorous prowess. Most of those trading and driving into it were short of women in the flesh and must necessarily build abandon in the imagination.

But Sebastian had a guest at his breakfast table. She wore no street dress, but a dancing gown, with a brilliant mantilla across her shoulders. This and the sleeplessness about her eyes was enough, even if Jim had not remembered face and gown and mantilla from the night before.

8

It was Dolores Portola who first saw him. She turned quickly, throwing one end of the mantilla up across her face as a veil. It was a useless precaution. She realized it and let the mantilla fall, watching him with a white, wooden expression. Sebastian looked up with no more evident a reaction than amusement at Jim's half-dressed appearance.

"Takes you a while to sober up, doesn't it, King?" he asked with mild disapproval. "You could have knocked."

"I did," Jim answered. "Three times—on your cook's scalp knot."

"Coffee?"

"No."

"Good for the nerves."

"Mine are fine."

Sebastian pointedly eyed Jim's exposed drawers.

"So I see. Steady as a rock."

He chuckled, then pointed up over the patio wall. "Seems to be a fire on the plaza."

"You ought to know. You set it." Sebastian glanced at the uneasy girl beside him.

"Hardly, King. Pay me the compliment of recognizing I have been too busy. It looks close to your store."

"That's where you wanted it, isn't it?"

Sebastian frowned a little.

"I wouldn't have bought you drinks last night if I had known I was also buying your bad manners this morning," he complained. "A pity you didn't sell your trappers' trade contracts last night when I offered to buy them. I'm afraid you don't have much to sell this morning."

"My accounts receivable," Jim answered.

9

"I thought you did only a cash business."

"I did, until this morning. There's just one uncollected account. An item of thirty-eight thousand dollars against you and Duval and Company for the merchandise and consigned furs you burned for me this morning. Payable in cash or trade goods—at St. Louis prices."

Sebastian smiled.

"You're talking about something impossible of proof."

"The fire?"

Jim's eyes touched the girl at the table.

"I don't have to prove that. Just where Señorita Portola spent the night. Her father and brothers will do the rest."

Horrified, the girl leaned sharply forward.

"You wouldn't do that!"

Jim looked grimly at Sebastian.

"Tell her, Luis—tell her there isn't anything I wouldn't do."

The man seemed a little shocked.

"A woman's honor—" he protested.

"A woman in your house has no honor, Luis. All three of us know that."

"Pig!" Dolores Portola gasped. "Dog!"

The expletives had no conviction. She was too frightened. Or ashamed. Jim could not tell. It really made little difference.

"Well?" he asked impatiently.

Sebastian slowly shook his head.

"No. Embarrassing to admit before the Senorita, it is true, but the price is too high. Perhaps it is worth thirty-eight thousand dollars to 'Lore to keep you from her father, but it is not to me."

The girl turned stricken eyes on Sebastian.

"You know my father—my brothers—I will be destroyed!"

"Nonsense," Sebastian answered easily. "Proper appraisal is a trader's art, 'Lore. I am quite sure of my estimate of values. Your father and your brothers are men. They have had women. They will know how little their precious merchandise has really been damaged. Embarrassing, as I said. That is all. The virtue of a saint is not worth thirty-eight thousand dollars."

The girl's shoulders hunched miserably together. Her mantilla fell away unnoticed. Agony was in her eyes.

"And you said so much that was different, last night—" she breathed.

"That was last night. Besides, our indecent *yanqui* friend is bluffing."

Dolores Portola was one of the belles of Santa Fe. She belonged to one of the proudest families. Jim had never heard her name mentioned with anything but respect, even in the camps of the roughest Yankee *caravaneros*. Her agony was real. He turned his eyes from her and locked gazes with Sebastian.

"All right, bluffing—but for the last time, Luis. I intend to collect that account in full."

Sebastian leaned back in his chair, making a precise little tent of his carefully tended fingers.

"You have already made enough trouble, Jaime, my friend. It must stop. To have a lot of friends does not necessarily mean that a man leads a charmed life."

"I was about to point out the same thing to you."

"You are now out of business. Stay out. Get yourself a pair of pants and get out of Santa Fe—for good!"

"A fair warning?"

"If you're entitled to one."

11

"I should be grateful for any kind of a warning, coming from you, Luis," Jim said dryly. "Thanks."

He turned and entered a hall which ran like a tunnel through the house from the patio to the street door. Dolores Portola followed after him, her heels clicking rapidly on the tile flooring as she tried to keep up with the long swing of his stride. He unbolted the door and stepped out onto the street. The girl touched his arm, stopping him. He glanced down.

"Better move along. Somebody's apt to see you."

"I've been a fool," she said swiftly. "But no more than a fool. Please believe that!"

"I wasn't too smart last night, myself."

"You would have told my father. For a little while you would have told my father."

"Yes. For a little while."

"I've been a fool and you've been a friend, Jaime King. I will remember."

"Fair enough," Jim said. "And I'll forget."

Her fingers tightened on his arm, then fell away. She hurried off up the Street of the Old Ones. Jim turned back toward the plaza.

CHAPTER 2

FRIENDS

WETZEL WAS NOT A HAPPY MAN. HE WAS BORN unhappy. He boasted of this often enough. The curse of an angry God was upon him and his. He boasted of this, also. He boasted of things which had price, and of price itself. He boasted of the harshness of a trade which left him no profit for his labors. But his misery was actually

12

a joy. Wetzel could not be happy except in being unhappy. It was a hell of a way of life, but apparently he liked it that way. He had to. It was all of his own doing.

Jim thought Wetzel was enjoying his persecution now. Jim wanted to think this. It made him feel better about the whole thing, about the rough companions who'd accompanied him into Wetzel's store. Mountain men, all.

Frontenac asked for the key to the padlock at the end of the long iron rod running through the trigger-guards of the weapons in the gun case and holding them secure against removal. Wetzel appeared not to hear him. He was watching in outrage as St. Vrain held a series of buckskin pants up to Jim King's belt line in an unsteady appraisal of fit. He was also trying to watch Kincaid rapidly shuffling through a rack of beautifully thin-scraped powderhorns so dexterously no eye could keep track of the battered old horn which he kept replacing with one and then another of those in Wetzel's stock.

Asking again with little insistence for the key and getting no answer—really wanting none—Frontenac seized the locked iron rod and pulled. Fronnie was a big man, uncommonly powerful, and the iron was softer than it should have been. It bent and pulled out of the trigger-guards of the racked guns like a length of limp legging-lacing. Wetzel moaned and Fronnie lifted out a pair of matched Allen and Thurber twin-barrels of rifle caliber and exquisite workmanship. They were the finest pistols in the case and might easily be the finest in Santa Fe. Fronnie sighted one at Wetzel, who ducked behind a hardware counter. St. Vrain shoved a pair of pants into Jim's hands.

"Put 'em on," he said. "You embarrass me. If they don't fit, wet 'em and shrink 'em to size. If they're good buckskin—"

He broke off as Wetzel's anguished features reappeared above the hardware counter.

"Good buckskin! They're the finest. Chewed soft and hand-sewn at San Juan. Two beavers a pair, they cost me!"

"Shoot him," St. Vrain said to Fronnie. "He's lying."

Frontenac snapped the aimed pistol.

"You'll ruin a good gun, dry-firing it like that," Jim said over his shoulder.

"Put on your pants before you teach me about guns," Fronnie said. "I ain't takin' lessons from anybody in diapers!"

Jim had the pants on now, and he stopped the whisky bottle as it came by from Monk Mooney. Fronnie had a bite, too.

"Here's to the bustedest bastards in the U.S.A.," Fronnie said.

St. Vrain deftly caught the bottle from Fronnie's big, careless hand.

"Gentlemen," he corrected gravely, "the bustedest gentlemen. Let us remember our dignity. What others call us is beyond our control, but let us be kind to ourselves. Kind and honest. Scrupulously honest."

He raised the bottle.

"Gentlemen—that's what we are!"

"Not me, Colonel," Fronnie protested. "I'm a bastard. A ring-tailed, side-windin', half-breed, Indian son of a bitch of a bastard, an' I can lick any man as says I ain't!"

"To see a comrade sunk so low," St. Vrain murmured sadly.

"Get out of here!" Wetzel shouted from the doorway. "Bums! Bandits! Get out of here!"

14

St. Vrain looked at Wetzel, one shaggy white brow rising.

"Bums?—Bandits?"

"Not you, Colonel," Wetzel said hastily. "Not you, sir!"

"My friend, Mr. King, perhaps?" St. Vrain asked sofly.

"Not him, either," Wetzel said reluctantly. "Outfitting him, ain't I? Best in the house—for nothing, yet!"

"And willingly?" St. Vrain prompted.

"Willingly," Wetzel agreed miserably. "Please, Colonel—"

"All right. Let's get out of here." St. Vrain headed for the door. Jim followed him. Fronnie came along, bringing the pair of Allen and Thurber pistols. Kincaid passed two of the best of Wetzel's powderhorns to Mooney and picked up the whisky bottle, nursing it tenderly. Mooney snagged a fat Hudson's Bay blanket as they passed a rack near the door.

"Try and get a grubstake!" Wetzel shouted after them.

"Try and get our trade!" Fronnie roared in answer from the walk.

They angled directly across the rutted, dusty plaza. There were a number of idlers and a few promenaders. These miraculously cleared from the square ahead of them. St. Vrain reached under his coat and proudly produced a well-made Mexican belt and possibles pouch. He handed them to Jim.

"Sometimes I worry about my honesty," St. Vrain said.

Jim grinned.

"Anything for a friend, eh?"

"Friend?" St. Vrain snorted. "I lost about eight thousand dollars in furs this morning because of a

15

misplaced trust in you. I need advice. Good advice. From my partner, His Excellency, the Governor."

He looked archly on across the plaza.

"I see no reason for his new duties to interfere with those of friendship," he went on. "We shall ask his opinion."

"About what?" Jim asked.

"As to whether we should hang you now or wait until sundown and charge admission."

He seized Jim's arm and steered him toward the main door of the *Palacio del Gobernador*. Behind them, Kincaid spoke warmly.

"Ol' Saul ain't a bad sort, is he? Outfittin' Jim complete, like he done?"

"Real generous," Fronnie agreed.

"Fit to ride the river with," Mooney added with a quaver of sincerity.

A servant sweeping before the *palacio* saw them coming and fled within. St. Vrain paused before the closed door and eyed the others uncertainly.

"As your superior officer—" he suggested.

"I could whip you if you'd take off your uniform, Colonel," Fronnie announced confidently.

"You and what two tribes of Indians?" St. Vrain asked scornfully. "When they get around to issuing uniforms to my New Mexico Militia, I'll give you a chance."

"Fronnie'd beat your brains out, Colonel," Monk said.

He pointed at the door.

"Go ahead—knock."

St. Vrain rapped on the door. In a moment a very handsome woman opened it. St. Vrain removed his hat with a flourish and an unsteady but graceful little bow.

16

"Colonel St. Vrain's compliments to the Governor, ma'am, and will he kindly get to hell out here?"

The woman frowned, but her eyes were laughing.

"Ceran St. Vrain, you're drunk!"

"You have spies," St. Vrain accused. "Illegal warfare, Carlita!"

Jim King had no idea what Mrs. Bent's real name was. Ceran St. Vrain had always called her Little Charlie—the power behind Big Charlie, her husband. The Spanish name had stuck in the trade.

Carlita Bent laughed, for she loved her husband's business partner as her husband did—as every man in the mountains did.

"War, between us—on a Sunday afternoon?"

"Civic duty," St. Vrain assured her.

He held tightly to Jim's arm.

"This man burned a fortune in furs belonging to us. We're going to hang him. Dangerous criminal, Carlita."

"Stole them pants," Frontenac said severely.

"Guns, too," Kincaid added.

"And a blanket," Monk said, waving the Hudson's Bay over his own arm. "From poor ol' defenceless, Saul Wetzel. In broad daylight."

Carlita Bent turned to Jim.

"I'm sorry about the fire. It really was set deliberately?"

"Sebastian didn't deny it."

"He wouldn't deny his father was the devil," Mooney said.

"Hang him, too," Frontenac proposed happily. "I could whip him if he didn't always keep a couple of knife-toters, with him."

"Only two, ain't they?" Monk asked scornfully.

"You're gettin' old, Fronnie," Kincaid said, dropping

17

his arm over Frontenac's massive shoulder. "Only two. Ain't like it used to be when me an' you—"

"We want to see Charlie, Carlita," St. Vrain interupted.

"He's sleeping, Ceran," Mrs. Bent said. "He was up very late last night and the fire turned him out early this morning. He went back to bed for a nap."

"Charlie's gettin' old, too," Kincaid mourned.

"Got to see Charlie," St. Vrain insisted. "Matter of life and death. Jim's life and death. We got to hang him."

"Hasn't enough been done to Jim for one day?" Carlita Bent asked, a little sharply.

"Make a man of him yet," Frontenac said.

Jim looked across the plaza at the burned-out front of the King Trading Company. Kids of three races were darting in and out, carrying off the smoked and scorched remnants of his stock as trophies. He wondered what kids did with the junk they seized and carried off so bravely. And he felt the sincere sympathy of the govenor's wife. It touched him and he felt sorry for himself. He guessed he was drunk again. He was glad he had his pants on now. It was more dignified.

"Got to see Charlie," St. Vrain repeated.

He stood very stiff and military, steadying himself on Jim's arm. Carlita Bent shrugged helplessly.

"All right, Ceran. Come in. I'll have Lupe heat you up some coffee and dip you some soup. I'm sure none of you have eaten. Charlie will be waking up pretty soon."

"I'm irresistible!" St. Vrain said triumphantly.

"Yes, Ceran—you're irresistible."

Mrs. Bent laughed and took his free arm.

"You always have been, to me. Come on."

"Wait a minute, ma'am," Monk said. "Ain't the third window yonder Charlie's?"

He pointed down the block-long veranda.

"Fifth," Kincaid said, squinting.

"Sixth," Frontenac corrected.

"Which?" Monk demanded.

"I don't know," Mrs. Bent answered.

"Kind of important, ma'am."

The governor's wife stepped farther out onto the veranda and carefully counted.

"The fourth, I believe," she said after a moment.

Monk drew his belt gun with a flourish which did not diminish the speed of the action. The gun slammed. Glass went out in the fourth window. Monk blew on the breech nipple of the weapon and cleared its barrel of smoke. He spoke then to Carlita Bent.

"Better have your woman dish up some soup for Charlie, too. I think he just woke up."

"Time he did!" St. Vrain said indignantly. "Town's getting disorderly. Open gunfire on the streets!"

He took Jim's arm with one hand and Carlita Bent's with the other, and steered them into the *palacio*.

It was very good soup. Jim had two bowls. And the coffee was strong enough to be an effective antidote even to *aguardiente*. Off in the residential portion of the house there was a considerable uproar. It subsided presently. When Mrs. Bent reentered with her husband, only a grimness about the mouth betrayed the fact that the Governor of New Mexico was still an angry man. He slammed down into a chair beside Ceran St. Vrain.

"All right," he growled. "What do you want?"

"For you to get off your hindside and do something about Luis Sebastian," St. Vrain said.

19

Charlie Bent eyed the others at the table. Jim watched him. He suddenly realized Bent's hatred for the appointment with which he had been saddled. His home was north, at Don Fernandez de Taos, not at Santa Fe. The big trading company he had founded with Ceran St. Vrain sprawled along almost one whole side of the plaza at Taos. The governorship separated him from his home and his business, both of which he loved. It separated him from his friends. He could no longer be as close as he once had been to these men now about his table. He turned finally to Jim.

"Sebastian was responsible for your fire?"

"I can't prove it."

"And yet you expect me to do something?"

"If you don't, Charlie, I will."

Bent shoved his booted feet far under the table and hunched down stubbornly in his chair.

"I won't do anything. Not without proof of something. And if I can help it, neither will you, Jim. You nor anybody else. Not without proof. Even if I have to lock the lot of you up."

"Including me?" St. Vrain asked incredulously.

"You'd be the first," Bent answered bluntly. "I know you best. None of you are going to make trouble."

"We ain't trouble-makers, Charlie," Frontenac protested in a hurt voice. "You know that. We just don't like Luis Sebastian, is all. Him an' that St. Louis outfit he works for."

"We got rights, Charlie," Monk Mooney added.

"So have a lot of other people," Bent answered wearily. "Yours are no more important than theirs. General Kearney appointed me governor because I'm supposed to have some influence over you—the trappers and traders and the rest of the damned white

20

Indians in buckskin pants out here."

"Charlie, listen," St. Vrain said earnestly. "Jim said he'd take care of his own burned fingers from that fire this morning. Forget the fire then. Forget Sebastian had anything to do with it. But this is important. Duval and Company is trying to tie up every penny and pelt of trade west of the Red and south of the Arkansas. Nine millions went over the trail last year. That's worth something."

"Competition," Bent said. "That's healthy. If you and I don't know that, who would?"

"Competition?"

St. Vrain angrily jerked his chair around.

"What kind of competition is this? Farady's dead—murdered in his own bed. His stock of goods foreclosed by Sebastian on a note Farady's widow swears he never signed. And it takes luck these days to get any wagons but a Duval string through the Comanches east of Glorietta. What's more, the raids are getting worse. Now Jim's burned out here. Who's that leave? Wetzel, and Sebastian's Duval and Company store!"

"There's still the two of them—Wetzel and Sebastian. That's competition."

"A blind," Mooney rumbled angrily. "Saul'd be ten times easier to shove out of the way than either Farady or Jim King. He ain't even been nudged. Only one answer to that. He's doing business for Duval under his own trademark."

"That—or he just isn't doing enough business to make any difference," Jim suggested.

"Hogwash!" Mooney snapped.

But Jim was without enthusiasm. He wanted to feel that with his own anchor in Santa Fe gone with the fire, there still remained one post open in defiance of

21

Sebastian and the Duval company. One channel of free trade. Wetzel was it.

"I'll tell you something, Charlie," St. Vrain said. "You think you're snug here in the *palacio*. You and Carlita. You think you're the government. You think that if Sebastian and the Duval outfit make an open bad move, you'll have them. So you aim to just wait for that. It'll be too late then, Charlie. Don't forget that nine millions over the trail—all theirs, if they can get it. And they know you. They won't wait for you to move, like you're waiting on them. They'll move first. They'll move right in here—right into the *palacio*. They'll heave you out and set up their own governor."

"They can't arrange that this side of Washington. Takes time. And I have friends there. I'd find out, the first move. Besides, they're welcome, if they do it that way. Ask Carlita if I want to be governor."

"I know, I know!" St. Vrain said impatiently. "I remember how you bellowed when General Kearney put the government brand on you. But I'm not talking about Washington, Charlie. I'm talking a lot closer to home and a lot plainer. I'm talking bullets. It doesn't take a bullet any time at all to remove a man from office. Do you have to sit and wait for that?"

Carlita Bent paled perceptibly, but she remained motionless and silent. Jim King was startled. He had never before associated fear with Charlie Bent's wife. She had always seemed one of the strong ones—as much a part of the mountain legion as any man present. But she was afraid. A cold, uncommunicating fear which could not have been generated just by St. Vrain's single statement of predicted violence. Jim felt hers was an old fear, nursed a long time. Her husband's partner had only nudged it, like treading on an almost forgotten

22

foot wound.

Jim thought St. Vrain had gone too far. So did Bent. The governor surged angrily to his feet.

"That kind of talk stops right now, Ceran!" he said sharply. "Do you think you're the only man in Santa Fe talking bullets? Do you think you're the only one talking of the millions that traveled eastward out of here last year? It's not like you to be a fool. And you haven't got any idea of what my job really amounts to!"

He swung to include the others, begging them also to know what he was trying to tell his partner.

"You know the story of the Dutch boy, trying to save all of Holland with his finger rammed into the dike? Well, I've got mine rammed into a barrel of powder!"

He crossed abruptly to one of the deeply recessed plaza windows. He looked out through this for a moment, then turned his back to it and faced the room. Jim noticed that in doing so he stepped instinctively a little to one side, so that the thick 'dobe wall rather than the paned window was actually behind him. A tilt of his head indicated the plaza.

"There are men out there who hate us. Men who were hating occupants of this building before our government was born. Big men and little men—Spanish and Mexican and Indian. Five of my friends can't drop in to see me of a Sunday afternoon—like you're doing now—without a hundred tongues wagging that the Yankees are plotting some new browbeating for them. And they believe it.

"Sebastian is Spanish. Claims to be, at least. They believe that, too. I'm not moving against him or the outfit he works for until I have proof every Indian and mestizo and *hacendado* in the territory can understand. I can't move against him any other way. I don't dare."

23

Bent pushed out from the wall and recrossed to St. Vrain.

"My job is to make friends. I'm going to keep the government and you and anyone else from making us one more enemy than we already have. You're going to help me or take the consequences—all of you!"

St. Vrain looked at his partner for a long time, then stretched out his hand, clamping Bent's shoulder.

"Sure, Charlie," he said earnestly. "I'll help. We all will. Everything we can—anything you say."

Bent looked at the floor.

"I hope you're not being damned fools, right along with me," he murmured.

"Wouldn't be the first time," St. Vrain said, grinning. "Don't take it so hard."

He dropped his hand and smiled at Mrs. Bent.

"Put him back to bed, Carlita. Take good care of him. He's an important man, these days. If that finger of his ever slipped—"

Charlie Bent looked up then. His lips curved in a tired smile.

"Ah, you go to hell!"

"If I do, I'll know where to look for company," St. Vrain told him.

He nodded to the others. They said good-by to the governor and his wife and filed out. St. Vrain halted Jim under the *palacio* veranda.

"Didn't get you much official help, Jim," he said.

"Re-outfitted me, at least. More than I deserve. Charlie's right, Colonel. He can't do much—now."

"He won't, anyways. So where's that leave you?"

Jim shrugged.

"Charlie can't do anything. You fellows—the rest of the legion—can't, either. With all the furs you gave me

24

on consignment gone up in smoke, the fire's left you as broke as I am. You'll all be scrabbling to get squared around before winter sets in. And I'll have to do something myself. Looks like I'll have to leave Sebastian be."

"Quit—you?" Mooney couldn't believe it.

"Now isn't that a hell of a question, Monk?" Jim grinned. "If I can't tackle Sebastian, I'll have to go after the man he works for."

"Duval?" Kincaid said sharply. "All the way to St. Louis?"

"Know anybody that'll lend me a horse?" Jim asked.

CHAPTER 3

St. Louis

JIM KING PAUSED WITHIN THE DOOR OF THE Fontaine, finding pleasure in the warmth and the smell of cooking. With the lowering of the afternoon sun, a chill was rising from the river, and he had come a long way from Santa Fe to St. Louis. A girl, wearing a thin, cheap cotton dress which fit her like her skin and held her breasts unnaturally high, weaved out of the crowd and linked her arm in his.

"You come with Flora, big man," she said. "Flora will find you a good table. Flora will be good to you."

"For nothing?" he asked dryly.

She let go of his arm and backed away a step, eyes flashing scornfully. He saw she was half Indian. Most of the river girls were part Indian—or Negro or Cajun or Spanish. Their season was short, for the mud of the river soon engulfed them. But while their bloom was fresh,

25

they were often quite beautiful. This one was no exception. Jim made the sign of empty pockets. The girl eyed him a moment more, then laughed uncertainly.

"You make the joke," she said, as she swung in beside him. Suddenly her hands darted out—to his chest and the two big breast pockets of his buckskin jacket—to his waist, where a money belt might be hidden—to his thighs, where some men wore secret inner pockets for their money. It was the deft work of an instant and gave her sufficient proof he was not lying. His pockets were empty. She spat at him and vanished among the crowded tables.

A man came in from the street behind Jim. He saw the girl's scornful departure and laughed at it. Jim turned to see a small, dapper, fashionably turned-out figure without a trace of the eternal mud of St. Louis. A man with a soft, delicately colored woman's complexion, small-boned woman's hands, and a figure which would have been feminine in its slenderness were it not for the instant knowledge it was fashioned of spring steel. Aside from the coloring, there was nothing feminine in the metallic eyes or the chill, handsome features. The man had an obvious idiosyncrasy. Instead of the weighted stick or the light sword cane such dandies usually fancied, he carelessly carried a beautifully mounted rifle as light in bore and frame as a toy. He pushed past Jim, still chuckling at the floor girl's abrupt departure, and moved on toward the bar at the far end of the room. Scowling a little, Jim followed him.

Near the bar a truculent looking man with a blue veined nose and an air of affluence occupied a table with one of the house girls. The man with the rifle tapped him on the shoulder with the barrel of the gun, much as someone else might have used a cane. The big

26

man and his girl companion swiveled around. No word was spoken, no signal given, yet they both hastily arose and left the table. The man with the rifle sat down. Jim passed on and halted against the bar a few feet away.

There were three dimes in Jim's pocket. He put one of them down on the bar and soon drank with relish his first eastern whisky in four and a half years. The drink was foolish, of course. It only made him the hungrier. But he wasn't going to get a hell of a lot out of his thirty cents, at best. It might as well be whisky. He turned with the glass in his hand.

Across a corner of the room, raised half a dozen feet above the main floor, there was a balcony-like addition with space for five or six tables. These were covered with linen. The chairs at them were upholstered. And so were their occupants. Here sat the titans of the River— the rulers of the fur trade—the millionaires of St. Louis. Alexandre Berthold—one of the Choteaus—a cousin of the numerous Pratte dynasty—Jim had no difficulty locating the man he was seeking among them. Edouard Duval was dark, heavy beyond normal obesity, and in complete command of the grand manner. He occupied the best table on the balcony, alone. It was obvious that others in this section, as well as the rest of the Fontaine, measured their own stature by the proximity of their tables to Duval's.

There was a compelling attraction to the man. And not because of his appearance. In fact, he was markedly grotesque. His almost spherical head was completely bald, even to the lack of brows and lashes on his puffy, heavy lidded eyes. His small mouth was out of proportion in his large round face. The tiny hands and feet at the extremities of his massive body were equally out of proportion. But his sureness was monumental.

27

Jim thought it was this which commanded the respect of the others. This and the man's coldness. He was completely devoid of any vestige of warmth. A body without a soul.

A group of housemen came from the rear and ousted two parties from tables on the main floor, directly in front of Duval's position on the balcony. They pushed the vacated tables together, forming a platform. When this was done, the tubercular man on the pianola contrived a surprisingly effective fanfare. Under cover of this, a girl emerged from the same door as the housemen and moved toward the improvised platform.

Jim rang down another dime. When he turned back with his refilled glass, the girl was up on the platform. She had slipped out of the loose cloak she had worn through the crowd and he saw that what he had thought was the hood of the cloak was actually a loose, sack-like mask, effectively concealing her from the shoulder line up. From the shoulder line down, little was concealed, and all that was visible ran into fluid motion as the pianola began to clatter again.

Well aware that he had been long in the mountains and subsequently in Santa Fe, where this kind of entertainment was not usual—well aware, in fact, that his judgment of the feminine might well be a bit rusty— Jim still thought he had never seen a body as beautiful as that of this dancer. And grotesque as her affectation of the hooded mask was, it was provocative. Having seen the body, a man wanted to see the face.

The girl's dance seemed to be for Edouard Duval. Jim could see the oily sweat begin to glisten on the man's face and on the obscene baldness of his scalp. Duval was spilled back in his chair, but there was tenseness rather than indolence in his sprawl. And his eyes did not

28

once leave the sinuous body before him. Jim watched the man more than the girl, considering the errand that had brought him to St. Louis—the collection of thirty-eight thousand dollars from the head of Duval & Co.

The dance came to an end. The girl wrapped herself in her cloak and stepped down to the floor. Thunderous, ribald applause shook the Fontaine. In the entire crowd, only three men did not join in the ovation. Duval heaved forward in his chair, leaning against his table, but only to follow the dancer's exit with avid eyes. Jim sipped his drink. The third man was the dandy at the table near the bar. He caught Jim's eye and motioned him over. With the end of the dance two waitresses had descended on the table with steaming trays. As Jim approached he saw they were setting two places.

"Hungry?" the dandy asked.

"I could eat a dog raw" Jim conceded.

"Will hump-rib do?"

The dandy reached his foot under the table and kicked out the chair at the second place the waitresses were setting.

"Sit down. Join me."

Jim dropped into the chair, eyeing the magnificent hump-rib buffalo roast now uncovered on the table. Char-broiled over a campfire, such a cut was second only to beaver tail among the gourmets of the buckskin legion. Cooked, as now, by expert chefs, with seasonings and side dishes impossible on the trail, it was one of the great delicacies of the table world. Jim's host expertly cut a two-inch slice and served his guest. Jim started eating immediately. The dandy smiled and began to eat, too. There was silence between them until Edouard Duval heaved to his feet and passed by them on his way out of the Fontaine. Jim half rose as the man

29

passed. He had come here intending to corner Duval and make his demand in public. However, it seemed more important to eat now. St. Louis was Duval's town. He would not be hard to find later on. Jim sank back down. Duval vanished through the street door.

"Just what is your business with our fat friend?" the man across the table asked quietly.

Jim looked blankly back at him.

"You've been watching him ever since you came in," the dandy said. "Even when La Fleur was dancing. There's a reason when a man does that. What is it?"

Jim studied his companion for a minute. There seemed no point in secrecy. Chances were all St. Louis would know why he was here soon enough, anyway.

"He owes me some money."

"How much?"

"Thirty-eight thousand dollars."

Jim's companion deftly dabbed a napkin at his lips, his brows rising at the sum.

"A legal debt—you hold a note for it?"

"No."

"Think he'll pay it?"

"I know he will. I've come all the way from Santa Fe to see he does."

"Somebody owes me some money," the dandy said thoughtfully. "A few thousand. Might as well be Duval as anyone else. Might as well make our collection together."

"What do you mean, might as well be Duval?" Jim asked.

"Very simple. I'm broke. Stony. Somebody has to contribute. Why not Duval?"

Jim stared at the man. The handsome face broke into a smile.

"I suppose I should introduce myself. My name is Tommie Defoe."

Jim stiffened, incredulous. Even in the mountains and Santa Fe, the name of Tommie Defoe was almost as well known at is was along the big rivers.

Tommie Defoe was dishonesty and death. A gambler who never lost at a turn of cards. A duelist who never missed. An unprincipled, deadly opportunist who had killed more men than Joseph had brothers. The rifle, Jim realized, should have been a tip-off, for this was Defoe's weapon. His marksmanship and incredible speed were as talked about as his name itself. But Jim pictured an arrogant, quarrelsome bully, not this quiet and fastidious little man. He was not the kind of killer painted by the legends which had reached Santa Fe. Jim searched for an answer and could find none better than his own name.

"I'm Jim King."

"I know," Defoe nodded. "Most people along the river know as much of you as they do of me these days. You and Colonel St. Vrain and Frontenac. Somebody's sure to recognize you as I did. The price of fame, King. By tomorrow all St. Louis will know you are here. Duval will know, if he doesn't already. And he'll know why. He won't give you a chance to tell him. A man doesn't get as rich as Duval by waiting for the other fellow to make the first move."

"Suits me," Jim said. "Let him make the move, then. Let him show his stripe. I'd like it that way."

"No." Defoe shook his head. "You wouldn't like it one damned bit. His first move will be your last. This isn't Santa Fe, where you've got friends. This is St. Louis. All friends here belong to Ed Duval. If you're going to collect what you think he owes you, you're going to have to do it tonight. And you're going to need help."

"You?"

Defoe shrugged.

"I told you I'm flat. Duval's money will spend as easily as anyone else's. Between the two of us we might do it. Duval doesn't trust banking houses. Why should he? He's bigger than any of then. He runs his own bank from the house."

"I'm no robber!"

"I can see that," Defoe said. "And you're also no businessman. Not the way business is done here."

His smiled widened. He lifted a piece of meat on his fork.

"Good roast, don't you think?"

CHAPTER 4

ENEMIES

THE SUMMONS CAME AT A LATE HOUR. THOUGH SHE had been waiting for it since she had returned from the Fontaine to her dressing room, Toni Bandelier was startled by the knock on her door. With her hooded mask already in hand, she crossed to the tiny peephole in the door panel and peered out. Seeing only Joe Skeen, she tossed the hood aside and shot the wooden bolt. Skeen came in and closed the door with his shoulders.

"The fat toad bit just like I told you he would," Skeen said. "He wants you—tonight."

"All right," Toni said.

"Half of what you get," Skeen reminded her. "And don't try to hold out on me. Mister Duval and me have

32

our understanding. Sooner or later he'll tell me what you cost him. It won't pay to cheat."

"I never cheat," Toni said. "Why should I?"

"Know the house?"

"I'll find it."

"Just don't let anybody see you. Mister Duval hates talk. Bad for his business."

"Or his pride," Toni suggested

"Business. He only thinks of business. If there's talk, he's hard to deal with. You be careful."

Toni nodded. She picked up her hood and her cloak and reached for the door latch. Skeen shook his head and stopped her.

"You're beautiful," he said regretfully.

"If I wasn't, Duval wouldn't have sent for me."

"And you're just a kid."

"He likes that, too."

"Look," Skeen said suddenly, "if you're broke I could let you have a few dollars."

"No."

"You don't have to do this. It's a hell of a way to make a stake. I've seen some of the others when they come back."

He ran the tip of his tongue over his thick lips.

"Stick to the regular trade, kid. Or maybe I could get you a job up-river at St. Joe. That masked dance of yours ought to go good up there. And no Duval making a claim."

"Good old Joe," Toni said to Skeen. "You think of that now. Kind of you—and makes your conscience feel better, doesn't it?"

Skeen shrugged rounded shoulders and ran appraising eyes over her.

"No skin off my nose. Suit yourself. But hold him up

for a hundred, at least. And get it in gold. You're the best I've ever sent him."

Skeen moved aside from the door and Toni pulled it open, stepping into the narrow, evil-smelling back hall of the Fontaine. At the far end of this another door let her out into the night. A single warped plank lay across the hog-wallow of Skeen's back yard. She negotiated this carefully, reached a dryer slope, and began to climb for higher ground. The unworn turf of the slope was firm and clean; she had no intention of arriving at her rendezvous with the mud of St. Louis on her feet.

As she climbed the St. Louis bluff, she kept her hand tight against the hilt of a knife in the folds of her cloak—a dozen inches of steel, tapering to a needle point. A weapon small enough to be concealed in her cloak, but powerful enough to kill a man—even a fat one.

Walking along a rutted road which led past the mansions of the great trading families, Toni counted off the houses in passing. Two belonging to the Choteaus. The Manuel Lisa place. The Berthold estate. The palace of the Prattes.

The last in the imposing row was the vast Cabannes place. And just short of this was the gateway of the house belonging to Edouard Duval. His name was on a brass plate against one gate pillar. Unlike most of the others, his house was set far back, as though repelling even casual interest. Equally unlike the others, the intervening space was in carefully tended landscape and garden. Late as the season was, first frost had not yet come and the scent of lingering blossoms drifted over the high wall. Toni stood in the road and looked in through the arched and grill-enclosed gateway toward the distant house.

In her mind's eye, she built another house beside this one. A well-remembered house, standing tight against its neighbors on a narrow street in the Vieux Carré. Not the best house in New Orleans, if the fortunes of owners were to be considered. Maurice Bandelier had never been one of the great millionaires. Perhaps because he had loved a good life too well to devote his energy to money alone. Perhaps because he was not so shrewd a businessman as some of his neighbors. It really made no difference. Certainly not now. What counted was that he had been a man to love.

Standing in the Missouri night, staring at the house before her and at the house in her mind's eye, Toni Bandelier could not understand her mother. Toni had been born in New Orleans. Now she had seen St. Louis. She had lived under the same roof as her father. Now she had seen Edouard Duval. She had been raised in the house in the Vieux Carré. Now she could see the Duval place. And there could be no choice. It seemed incredible that a woman could leave Maurice Bandelier and the house in the Vieux Carré and New Orleans for this.

It had been long ago. Her father had been dead for six years now. The last of his dwindled estate had been sold off the past spring by agents to satisfy Duval & Co. for the Bandelier debts they had bought and discounted. And it had been nearly ten years since her mother, Madelon Bandelier, had slipped from the house in New Orleans and vanished into up-river mists with a dowry of twenty thousand dollars of her husband's gold and a man whose name no one had heard before.

Ten years ago this house before her now had not existed. In fact, her mother had never occupied it, for Madelon Bandelier had died while it was building. Ten years ago Edouard Duval had no fortune of his own, only twenty thousand dollars stolen by a faithless woman from a man who loved her. And ugly as St. Louis was now, it must have been far uglier ten years ago. No, Toni did not understand her mother. She only hated her.

It was not a hatred to be softened by news of Madelon's death, by her own hand, in an upper room of a log hotel in St. Louis, so the vague report went. The night the news came, Maurice Bandelier did not come home. He was found in the wash of the levee the next day. So the River had claimed him and Toni hated the River, also. She hated it as she hated her mother and Edouard Duval. A consuming hatred, fused with the same fierce pride which had made her La Fleur when the last of her money was gone, but which would not let her dance in public unmasked.

Sound came to Toni as she stood staring at the gates of Duval's house. The slogging footfalls of men on the bluff road. She ducked across to the gate, intending to take shelter in the arch. She did not touch the grille, but the gate swung silently open. Slipping through this she reclosed it, huddled in the shadow of one of the pillars, and hastily drew on her hood. The footfalls came on along the road and passed the gate. A pair of masculine silhouettes—one tall, broad-shouldered, free moving—the other small, slender, treading the mud underfoot with aversion. When they were past, Toni turned up the garden footpath toward Duval's house. As she did so a bulky shadow moved from a near-by bush and a hand gripped her arm.

"You are prompt," Duval said. "I like that."

Toni made no answer. They moved in silence to the

house. Duval freed her arm to select a pair of keys from a chain-hung ring. Using these, he opened the double lock but checked her as she would have passed through the door ahead of him. She understood in a moment. Two huge dogs were chained in the entry. Duval crossed to them, shortening their chains, then motioned for her to enter.

Both beasts strained against the shortened chains, eyes fastened upon her and powerful bodies corded, but they made no sound. Motioning her further back into the hall and keeping himself between the dogs and his guest, Duval freed both animals and turned them out through the open door into the night. They went with great bounds, but silently, still. Duval closed the door and employed both keys to refasten the locks. As he turned back to Toni he negligently kicked the chains to which the dogs had been fastened back against the base of the wall. Since he could not see her face, Duval appeared to assume her fear of the dogs—perhaps because he had seen it in others and expected it now.

"The dogs are merely a guarantee of privacy," he said. "They'll roam the garden till daylight and they'll kill any living thing they find inside of the wall or outside of the house. We won't be disturbed, but you must be sure to let me know when you wish to leave."

"Yes," Toni said, understanding the warning perfectly. "Yes, I'll let you know."

"I am proud of the dogs," Duval went on. "They make no sound, you noticed. They kill with no sound."

"What did you do to them?" Toni asked.

"Training," Duval answered. "Beat them for every bark and whimper from the moment they were born. It is not difficult to train an animal. It requires only patience and a firm hand. I tell you this because it is necessary that you learn a little in order to be pleasant company to me. You may now remove your mask."

Toni looked about the bare hall, dimly lighted, with a broad, vacant stair rising to the silent upper floor. The smell of the dogs was strong in the air. She shivered.

"Presently," she said.

Her eyes were not on Duval and she did not see him move. She heard only the rustle of movement and felt the explosion of his open hand against her masked cheek, and suddenly she was on the floor, looking up into the placid face of the man standing over her.

"You may remove your mask," he repeated.

Toni had no fear of recognition. She had been ten the one time this man had seen her in New Orleans. A child. And in maturity no hated reminders of her mother were about her. She rose slowly and removed her hood, shaking out the released jet cascade of her hair. Duval smiled then with a satisfaction so open and unguarded as to be startling in a man Toni had already classified as dangerously devious in all things.

"Skeen has done well by me," Duval said.

He crossed the bare hall to a door, opened it, and stood aside for Toni to precede him. She moved into a room of unusual elegance and comfort. A fire crackled in a massive hearth set into one wall. It was flanked on either side by glass-enclosed bookcases which rose from the thick carpet on the floor to a ceiling lost in shadow. A large rosewood table sat on a four-legged pedestal of carved gargoyles in the center of the room. A litter of books and papers, an ink and sand stand, and a pair of small lensed, steel rimmed spectacles on the uppermost papers, covered the table top. Toni knew she was looking at the well-spring from which the affairs of Duval & Co. were directed.

There was an immense soft leather divan facing the fire, a deep chair facing the rosewood table, and a large iron safe to one side of the door by which they had entered the room. Behind the table was a square, heavily built work chair. There were no other seats. It was apparent Duval did not often enjoy the company of others. Or if he did, he did not entertain in this room.

Despite heavy draperies, now closed, Toni had a glimpse of iron barring on the inside of the windows. In a solitary corner wall space, near the safe, hung an indistinct and badly done portrait of a woman. Madelon Bandelier had been one of the great beauties of the lower river. It was possible to recognize her likeness, even in this unintentional caricature. Entering behind Toni, Duval saw her interest in this portrait. He shrugged a little.

"There have been many before you. She was the first. You'll forgive the sentimentality?"

He escorted her across to the divan, standing in wait for her cloak, but she deftly slid out of this unaided and placed it near her on the divan. Duval remained standing, back to the fire, as she seated herself.

"I trust you do not find this embarrassing, La Fleur— that is your name, is it not?"

"For tonight."

"Perhaps many other nights as well," Duval amended. "How many depends upon you. I spoke of embarrassment. None is necessary. Merely that you understand me. I am unlike any man you have ever known. This house is proof of that. The fortune which built it was forged of ambition alone. And ambition is nothing more than knowing what you want and getting it."

He paused, smiling.

"Vanity? It has the sound, but it is not. Unarguable fact, complete with proof."

His gesture swept the room.

"What ordinary men find in a woman, I do not want. Unfortunately, with due apology to you, women vary little. I must invent the unique and the unusual, much as the caliphs of the Orient were forced to invent to avoid eating of the same feast as the common man. And I must say that until now Skeen has sent me very little with which to work."

Duval crossed to a little cabinet, which he bent to unlock with another key at the end of a gold chain about his neck. His recurrent smile troubled Toni. Grotesque as the man was, the smile was pleasant, and, together with the quiet pleasantry of his manner, it made him capable of a not always repellent reptilian charm. He took two small crystal goblets and a decanter from the cabinet. Filling the goblets with a heavy, pale green liqueur, he carried one back to Toni.

"I never drink alone nor in public," he said. "A misfortune of determination, since I am fond of alcohol. But I imbibe only when I have a guest in the house. To you—"

He sipped and let the liquor lie sensuously upon his tongue before he spoke again.

"Like the blood of ancient princesses—a whole dynasty of the proudest and most beautiful women who ever lived—distilled into a single flask!"

Toni tasted the liqueur. It was exquisite and completely unknown to her. Duval drained his glass and refilled it, making no effort to hurry his companion. Drinking abruptly now, after that first sip, taking the whole goblet in a pair of greedy swallows, he twice refilled it again before returning to his place at the fire.

"I want no coquetry," he said without preface. "I don't want to be merely tantalized by temptation. I want to be torn by it—rent asunder—I want torment to match my will, so that my surrender will be an honorable defeat. That's what I want from a woman!"

Toni sipped her liqueur and looked at him without answering. Duval made another pilgrimage to the cabinet to refill his glass. He came back again to the fire.

"You will remove your clothing and repeat the dance you did tonight at the Fontaine. With the mask, if you like, since I now know what lies beneath it."

Toni saw a slight unsteadiness in his hands which had not been there before. Perhaps it was due to some special potency in the pale liqueur. Perhaps it was because this man was not so different from other men as he fancied he was. In either case, this unsteadiness was Toni's strength and she knew it. Very slowly and deliberately she started disrobing to the scanty costume she had worn in the Fontaine. As she disrobed she kept her cloak always within reach, and she thought of the ruin of Maurice Bandelier with an avidity matching that growing in Duval's heavy-lidded eyes as more and more of her body came to view.

CHAPTER 5

BUSINESS MEETING

THEY MADE A FULL CIRCUIT OF THE HIGH WALL surrounding the Duval place and returned to the entry gate on the bluff road.

"Cosy little place," Tommie Defoe said. "Trusts his

fellow man to the limit, doesn't he? No side gates—none at the back—just this one. Good thing your business, at least, is legitimate, King. Looks like we'll have to walk right in the front way."

"Not me," Jim said.

"Getting scruples again?"

"Maybe, but that isn't it. Duval knows we're out here—or that somebody is."

"What makes you think so?"

"For one thing, the gate isn't locked. just latched."

Defoe grinned.

"Practically an invitation. What's wrong with that?" he asked.

"He's turned his dogs loose since the first time we came past here, too."

"Dogs?"

Defoe tipped his head in a doubtful listening pose. Jim took his arm and moved him a little aside to give him a clear view through the gate. A swift, silently moving shadow shot across an open stretch in Duval's garden. Defoe sucked in his breath.

"Good Lord—big enough to drag down a buffalo! How many of them are there?"

"Two, I think."

Defoe shifted his rifle into both hands.

"I don't like killing animals. And I hate to send our card in to Duval ahead of us. But it looks like there's only one sure way—"

Jim stopped him.

"Give me your gun and see what you can do about climbing that gate pillar."

Tommie looked at the rough masonry pillar and passed the rifle to Jim. If Jim had any doubt of the small man's superb physical condition, it vanished now.

42

Utilizing crevices in the uncoursed masonry, Defoe climbed the pillar as effortlessly as he might a ladder, stretching himself out along the top of the wall. Jim passed the rifle up to him. The dogs, attracted by this threatened entry, ceased their ranging and bounded over, flinging themselves in silent ferocity against the gate and the base of the pillars. There were only the two Jim had spotted before. It seemed unlikely there were any more.

"Friendly," Defoe whispered from the top of the wall. "Nice playmates for children. But why don't they bark?"

"Ask Duval," Jim said.

He studied the house. It was dark except for a trace of light around two draped windows on the lower floor. He judged it would be difficult to gain entry to the house, but in any event they first had to get past the dogs.

"I'll open the gate," he said quietly to Defoe. "The minute the dogs are out through it, you drop down and close it again from inside—and be sure it latches tight. Leave your gun up there. I'll pick it up as I come over."

Tommie grunted not altogether approvingly. Jim backed a little from the gate, drawing the attention of the leaping dogs wholly to himself. Suddenly he rushed his side of the gate with a ferocity almost equal to that of the dogs. Taken aback, the animals retreated a pair of yards. In this moment of uncertainty, Jim tripped the latch of the gate and began his own retreat. Reaching the pillar, he scrambled frantically upward as the dogs hit the gate. The unfastened grille swung outward under the impact of their charge and the gate covered Jim for another necessary instant. He swung his heels high and flattened himself along the top of the wall, dislodging and barely catching Defoe's gun as it started to fall.

Defoe, on the ground, seized the gate and swung it closed before the dogs could turn. Jim dropped down beside him. The frenzied animals piled back against the grille, puzzled by the reversal of their position at the gate. One of them swung his head toward the distant river bottom lights of the town. Both quieted as though their duty had been done. In another moment they trotted off with amiable curiosity down the road toward the lights.

Defoe breathed a gusty sigh of relief. Jim grinned.

"Don't worry about them for a spell. Probably the first time they've been outside this wall since they were born. They'll take themselves a good long look at the sights of St. Louis."

"Know a lot about animals, don't you, King?"

"Why shouldn't I?"

"That's right—why shouldn't you? Animals have been your business—one way or another. I envy you."

"Why?"

"Your association with dumb beasts. So much more satisfactory than those I've known. Man isn't the most pleasant animal with which to associate."

"I've known a few I didn't mind."

"Men?"

Defoe grunted deprecatingly.

"Your good fortune, then. You and your mountain friends are a race apart, found only in the far reaches. I personally have an abiding dislike for my own species."

"What have you got against Duval?"

"He's rich and I'm poor. The best possible reason for hatred."

Defoe gestured toward the house.

"The sooner we equalize the difference between Duval and myself, the sooner I am back in funds again,

44

the sooner you're going to be able to improve my outlook on mankind in general."

"The hell with your outlook," Jim said.

He scowled. Tommie Defoe wore his vocabulary and his knowledge with the same precise, almost self-mocking air of perfection with which he wore his impeccable clothes—the same air with which he managed the affectation of the rifle he carried. It was hard to know how much of the rest of him—even to his reputation—was affectation, also.

They moved up the walk together, diverged from it, and passed under the windows which leaked light. The drapes were too tightly closed to afford even a peep within, and there was silence beyond them. Jim and Defoe slipped along the side of the house to the rear and came to a narrow back door, flanked by rubbish containers and a stench-ridden slop yard—the inevitable backside of elegance. This door was barred on the inside but its fit had been loosened by weather and much usage. Defoe produced a spring knife and snapped open the thin blade with a touch on the release button. He slid the blade between the door and the jamb. He worked for an interminable pair of minutes, then withdrew the blade and slipped it through the opposite jamb.

"Straight bar, clear across," he whispered. "Got it lifted free of one bracket. When I lift this other end clear, it's apt to fall and make a noise. Be ready,"

Jim nodded. Defoe's knife whispered in the crevice of the jamb, working upward on the weight of the bar within. Suddenly the bar fell free, making an unnaturally loud clatter. Defoe pushed on the door. It swung inward. Both of them darted through, flattening against the inner wall on either side of the doorway.

Sound came from close by. Sound like that of a

45

slumbering servant, stirring restlessly in his sleep. Jim put his hand out experimentally and encountered a stove, still slightly warm to the touch. The sleeper seemed somewhere beyond it. They waited a moment without motion. The unseen man's breathing remained regular and there was no more stirring, as though he had dropped back into deep slumber. Jim sensed Defoe in motion and moved with him. They reached a door in the opposite wall together. Jim tried the handle and found it worked freely. He pushed the door open and they stepped into the rear of a huge, vacant central hall. Jim picked up the scent of the dogs they had encountered at the gate, and he knew this was where they had been kept.

At the far end of the hall, off to one side of the front door, was another doorway. Light showed beneath it. They moved silently toward this. As Jim reached for the latch, Tommie Defoe eared back the hammer of his rifle. The lock of the weapon was so finely made that the sear made only a whisper of sound as it came to cock. Jim thrust on the door. The panel swung soundlessly inward, revealing a bizarre scene which lay across Jim's palate like an old and ugly taste.

The dancer from the Fontaine—the one whom Defoe had called La Fleur—was undulating before the wide hearth at the other end of the room, in the same hooded mask and scanty costume. But where the body had been beautiful in the crowded tavern, impersonal because of the presence of so many, it was evil and lascivious here, for only one man's eyes were upon it. Drenched in his own sweat, head cocked a little to one side as though to see better, Edouard Duval stood against the mantel, a small goblet of some pale drink in his hand. His glassy eyes followed every movement of the sinuous body

46

before him. And the movements were no longer a dance. There was no music, no rhythm, no intent to entertain. It was, instead, deliberate and calculated aphrodisia.

Although the hood masked her face, Jim could sense a malice in the dancing girl. A wicked delight in the unmistakable suffering of the man standing against the mantel. Duval's torment was obvious. He was deliberately, with enormous effort, restraining himself from seizing what was offered so mockingly and tantalizingly before him. This agony of denial, flogged to acute pitch by the undulations of the girl's body, was his pleasure and his delight and his ecstasy. Jim could not tell whether the girl realized this or whether she even cared. But he hated her for being party to it.

Reaching behind him, Jim swung the door shut. It closed with a sound that jolted like a cannonade in the room. The motion of the dancer's body ceased at a point off-balance and she had to take an awkward sidestep before her masked face swung toward the door. Duval started violently and the goblet in his hand broke and fell musically to the hearthstone. His heavy-lidded glassy eyes swung from Jim King to Defoe, then to the hand which had held the goblet. Pale liqueur dripped from his fingers and turned crimson from a cut in his palm. The man leaned back against the mantel and the sheen faded slowly from his eyes. La Fleur stepped quickly to the divan, caught up her cloak, and flung it about her.

"We'll make this as quick as possible," Jim said. "Both of you stay as you are."

He crossed the room, Tommie Defoe keeping abreast of him part of the way, then separating to round one end of the divan to face Duval.

"Open your safe," Tommie told the man softly.

Duval reached into the breast pocket of his waistcoat and produced a white kerchief. He wrapped this about his cut hand, knotting it deliberately with his free fingers and using his teeth to pull the knot tight. All of this time he ignored Jim and eyed Defoe appraisingly. He plainly knew the small man's name and reputation and was measuring many things against it. Suddenly his glance shifted to Jim.

"You're James King, aren't you—from Santa Fe?"

Jim nodded.

Duval smiled wryly.

"And Luis Sebastian thought you were through—that you had already had enough—that you wouldn't come here."

"Sebastian makes mistakes," Jim said.

"Very few."

"One is enough for me. You owe me thirty-eight thousand dollars, Duval. Pay it—now!"

"How convenient you know the precise figure."

"Open your safe," Defoe said again, prodding his rifle toward the hairless man's massive midsection.

Duval blinked at the gun, then at the man behind it.

"So I owe you something, too. What's your account?"

Defoe shrugged carelessly. He tilted his head toward La Fleur, standing near Jim.

"Say I'm her brother—willing to set a price on her virtue. If that doesn't suit you, invent an account of your own."

Duval turned back to Jim, his benign manner belied by the hardness of his eyes.

"This lawless entry sets poorly on you, King. You have a reputation for honesty."

"You haven't," Jim answered. "There are a lot of us

48

in Santa Fe besides Sebastian who know what you're trying to do—what you'd do to anybody who stood in your way if they gave you half a chance."

"Really?"

Duval's surprise was mocking.

"Quite remarkable, since I doubt if even Luis has any real conception of my eventual plans. Santa Fe—"

The man paused and closed his eyes for a moment.

"Santa Fe!—Santa Fe will be my town, King. It's a pity a few of you buckskin patriots insist on taking the principle of equal opportunity so literally!"

"It's a habit you get into in the mountain country. A lot of us have it. Including Governor Bent."

"So I understand," Duval agreed. "Regrettable. I could make a few of you—including yourself and the governor—very rich men."

"Charlie's already rich enough to suit him," Jim said. "I will be when I've collected what you owe me."

"Open your safe, Duval," Tommie Defoe said again.

Duval shrugged and pushed away from the mantel, starting toward the safe at the other end of the room. Defoe smiled and eased his rifle to follow the man. Jim also turned, eyes on Duval, thinking that perhaps Defoe had known the best way to transact business with the head of Duval & Co. after all. The thinking may have been right, but the turning was a mistake. There was a rustle of movement behind him and the needle point of a steel blade bit into the flesh of his back over one kidney. It was not a deep penetration, but no mere prick either. He understood the warning and stiffened and halted. The hooded girl reached from behind him and secured his belt gun, then snapped an order in French to Defoe. The words were too swift for Jim to understand them or their meaning.

Defoe wheeled, swinging his rifle up and around in a completely automatic but incredibly swift reaction. Jim's pistol fired in La Fleur's hand. Muzzle-flash stung Jim's arm. Defoe staggered and sprawled across the litter of papers and books on the table in the middle of the room. Duval, apparently as astonished as Jim himself, stood half turned, looking back toward the hooded girl with his heavy eyelids for once raised high.

Jim's subsequent movements were instinctive. Under cover of the shot he lunged aside twisting, and caught La Fleur's two wrists. He wrenched them simultaneously, catching his gun as it fell from her right hand. The slender knife she had held against his back fell from her left hand to the floor. Jim kicked the blade far under the divan and retained his grip on one of La Fleur's wrists, forcing the girl toward Defoe.

"Got to get out of here!" Defoe said hoarsely. "Whole damned house will be down on us now!"

Jim nodded. Controlling the girl by twisting her wrist, Jim half-supported Defoe and got him past Duval to the hall door. Here Jim suddenly threw La Fleur to the floor and jerked the door open. Defoe stepped through it, still clinging to his rifle. Jim slid after him and slammed the door behind them. Once in the hall, Tommie stepped clear of Jim's support and sprinted lightly with him to the rear. They darted through the kitchen—where they had heard the breathing of the sleeping man—but they were not challenged. A moment more and they were outside.

Running silently abreast they hit the front gate and let themselves out onto the bluff road. Near a second-growth thicket a hundred yards along, Jim halted and scowled back at Duval's yet silent house. There was no sign of alarm or pursuit. Jim wondered at this, then

50

turned accusingly to Defoe, who had seemed so hard hit, but who had managed himself in the escape from the house so well.

"I thought that girl nailed you!"

"Think I can afford to have it bandied about the river that Tommie Defoe was hit by a waterfront belly-wiggler? She missed me clean. But it seemed smart to let her think otherwise.

"She meant that shot as a warning—didn't intend to hit me. When she thought she had, it shook her up enough to let you get your hands on her. Besides, it was time to get out of there—without giving her another chance."

"Duval's going to believe you were hit, too." Jim said. "You had me fooled. He'll hunt us, for sure. There's nothing else to do now but head back to the grass. It was a waste of time to come here. I should have known better than to try to take Duval in his own country."

Defoe shrugged philosophically.

"A hazard of the game," he said.

He reached in his pocket and brought out a thin wad of bills.

"Half's yours. Must be a hundred or so apiece. Saw it on the table in there. That's why I fell across it. Probably laid out as a fee for La Fleur, in case she earned it. Go ahead and take the grass if you want. I'm heading for the river."

"Better come with me," Jim urged.

"Why?"

"Duval controls the river. That's the first place he'd look."

"That the real reason you want me with you?"

"Well," Jim said, grinning a little, "I owe you a dinner. The way it looks, I won't be able to repay you this side of Santa Fe."

51

"Sentiment," Defoe scoffed. "I'm mercenary, King. Talk money."

"There ought to be an honest dollar or two to hand out if I can get back in business in Santa Fe."

"No fun in honest money," the little man protested.

"There will be in this—if we make it."

Defoe cocked his head in wry self-appraisal.

"Tommie Defoe in Santa Fe? Me—in buckskin? Nobody'd believe it. Me, most of all!"

"Look, Defoe," Jim said. "Duval intends to make himself into a big man in Santa Fe. A bigger man than he is here. Now maybe I couldn't collect what he owes me here, but I sure as hell can out there, one way or another, and maybe kick him and his out of New Mexico Territory while I'm at it."

"That begins to sound a little more like it—profit and a fight in the same deal. Only one thing—while you're making your collection from Duval, I get to pass my hat, too?"

"For whatever the traffic will bear," Jim agreed.

"That's up to you."

Defoe gripped his hand.

"The grass it is then!"

CHAPTER 6

UNFINISHED BUSINESS

TONI LAY SPRAWLED WHERE THE TALL MAN IN BUCK-skin had flung her. She heard the footsteps of Tommie Defoe and his companion in the hall, clattering toward the rear of the house with more speed than she had imagined a wounded man could achieve. She was grateful for that. She had not meant to hit Tommie. And she hoped the wound was not too severe. Turning her head, she looked at Edouard Duval.

The trading titan's bulk seemed shrunken by the brief presence of tall Jim King in the room. And his stature had not returned with the buckskin man's departure. He stood staring back at Toni. He made no move, gave no alarm—he just stared, with his hand resting as though for steadiness on the disarranged table across which Tommie Defoe had fallen. His nostrils flared a little, as though sampling the odor of gunpowder in the air.

Toni thought again of the shot she had fired and her reaction to it. She had hurt Tommie, but he had been meddling as always, intentionally or not. She had shot him. She had done many things to men, but she had not known she could do this. She had mocked men and cajoled them and tormented them, but she had slept with none and she had not before drawn blood. She had not been sure she could kill. But now she knew. The knowledge gave her a queer, detached sureness—a feeling of power. Not that there was exhilaration in the violence of the act. She felt a little unsteady over that part of it still. But the physical courage, the instantaneous decision—this was important. It meant that she could indeed kill Duval as she had planned. It meant that henceforth she had more than her body to use. It made her more than a woman. Tommie of course could not understand this. There was no way to let him know. She wondered if he would understand if he did.

She looked at Duval and scrambled to her feet. Her glance shuttled once to the hall door. Duval shook his head.

"It is useless to give alarm," he said. "Only Rupert is in the house tonight, sleeping in the kitchen. He is stone

53

deaf. He will have heard nothing. He would not hear you now."

He paused with a slight shrug.

"Rupert is useful when I have guests—invited ones."

He straightened a little.

"That was Tommie Defoe. You shot him."

Toni nodded.

"Why?"

Toni shrugged.

"Excitement."

"You fence with words," Duval said. "I do not care for women who do so."

"They'll get away," Toni countered. "You don't care for that either, do you?"

"Those two? Unlikely. One with a bullet in him and the other with his pockets empty? No, they'll not get away. Tomorrow we think of them. Tonight we think of you."

"As you wish."

Duval's lips thinned impatiently.

"You evade me. You know what I mean. You were not obliged to interfere."

"No," Toni agreed. "No, I wasn't."

Duval walked slowly around the divan, eyes warily on her. Suddenly he bent and retrieved her knife from where Jim King had kicked it. He balanced the slender blade on his palm and smiled across at her without humor.

"It couldn't be that you were afraid they would not only rob me, but you as well?"

"I don't understand."

"It couldn't be that you were afraid Defoe and his buckskin friend would kill me before you had that pleasure yourself?"

"To kill is a pleasure?"

"Damn you, answer my question!"

"I was only afraid they would take all of your money—before you had paid me for tonight.''

Duval laughed. She knew he did not wholly believe her. He sauntered back to the table in the middle of the room, the knife still in his hand, and he used the point of the weapon to rummage through the disarranged papers there. His careless manner suddenly became more intent. He rapidly searched the table top, then straightened.

"Your fears are better grounded and your marksmanship less effective than I thought." he said. "I had two hundred dollars put out for you here—in case you earned it. It's gone. Defoe must have grabbed it while he pretended to fall here. Perhaps it will not be so easy to find our two callers tomorrow after all."

"You don't act like you much care."

"I don't," Duval agreed. "If they stay in St. Louis, I'll have them easily enough. If they take to the river, they'll wind up in Natchez or New Orleans. If they take to the country, they'll wind up in Santa Fe. King will see to that. Eventually I'll have them, wherever they go— Take off that damned hood!"

Toni obeyed. Duval studied her face intently for a long time, then crossed to the safe. He knelt there and dialed the combination. The door swung open. He reached inside and counted out a small stack of money. Rising, he extended it to her.

"Your fee. You've earned it."

Toni took the money and coolly recounted it. The total startled her.

"You're generous."

Duval laughed again.

"That's a belief I'm afraid you alone possess, my dear. This is merely fair reward for outstanding service."

He gestured toward the safe.

"See for yourself. If I had been forced to open that safe I would have lost a great deal."

Toni looked inside the strongbox. It was loaded with money. More money than she ever dreamed existed. Fat pouches and great heaps of it. She thought of the few bitter dollars she had been able to win by humiliation and debasement, and she measured all she could ever hope to accumulate against this treasure in Duval's safe. Suddenly she was glad he had not locked her, earlier in the evening, in the sickening embrace she had expected. Suddenly she was glad she had not been forced to see if she could actually use the knife now lying on the table in the center of the room. Suddenly she was glad she had not tried to kill Duval. She knew she could do so any time now, and she knew she could wait.

It wasn't that she hated the man less for what she saw within the safe. Actually she hated him more for the degree to which he had multiplied her mother's stolen dowry. But she knew now where his pride lay, and she had a vision of destruction she could relish far more than the death of his gross body. She smiled.

"I could shoot a man every night for three hundred dollars," she said.

Duval smiled back at her.

"I can't afford to have some of my enemies killed. But there's another way—"

He reached out and suddenly stripped her cloak from her, so that she stood once again before him in her brief dancing costume. He backed away a little, surveying her minutely and critically. After a long moment he

56

chuckled.

"I believe I would get more pleasure out of what you might do to certain of those enemies than I would from what you could do for me."

He paused, frowning.

"Can you be a lady—do you know anything about it?"

"Enough to resent the question."

Duval chuckled again.

"Can you keep yourself from getting involved?"

Toni strolled over to the table, picking up the knife and impudently thumbing its keen edge.

"I'm hardly man-crazy, if that's what you mean."

"No," Duval agreed. "Obviously not. Stupid of me to have asked."

He surveyed her critically again, then tossed her cloak back to her as suddenly as he had stripped it away.

"It grows late," he said. "I'm making a sacrifice, believe me. A personal sacrifice I regret extremely. But I have made sacrifices before for the sake of business."

He paused thoughtfully.

"That you have to understand, I think. You have to understand me. Little business everyone understands. But big business, it is not understood at all. No man owns a big business. Who would believe that? But it is true. No man owns a big business—it owns him. It sucks his blood. It eats his body. It steals his sleep. It makes everything he wants impossible to attain. It makes him lonely and fills him with self-hate. It drives him to strange pleasures which have no real pleasure in them. It makes him inhuman. But it grows. It gets bigger. Always bigger. That is the thing. No one can understand what it means—the bigness and the growing. Everything is sacrificed for that. Maybe it is worth it. I

57

believe it to be."

He tugged on his vest chain and drew out his keys.

"I am sorry to give you up, my dear. Truly sorry. You are the most beautiful of them all."

He unsnapped a key from the ring and handed it to Toni.

"You will find the south room at the head of the stairs quite comfortable, I think. I will waken Rupert and send him to Skeen. Skeen will know what to do. It is best La Fleur permanently disappear from St. Louis tonight. Tomorrow we will make plans for Mrs.—Mrs.—"

He broke off, searching for a name.

"*Miss* Palliard," Toni suggested.

"Palliard—excellent," Duval agreed. "But Mrs. Palliard. For your own safety and comfort. A wealthy young widow whose business interests take her to the metropolis of our newest territory."

Toni's eyes widened.

"Santa Fe?"

Duval nodded, smiling.

"Santa Fe—yes. Sleep well, my dear."

He opened the door into the central hall and stood aside for her to pass through it ahead of him.

A maid aroused Toni in the morning, bringing with her a body-shaped copper tub and a great woolly robe of toweling. She returned with another servant, laden with buckets of steaming water and Toni had her first bath outside of the muddy river itself since she had left New Orleans. With the confidence of a clean body, she wrapped the robe about her and descended the stairs.

The room in which her mother's portrait hung had been put back in order. The position of the big table in the center of the room had been straightened and its litter had been neatly rearranged. The drapes were pulled back wide and the sun streamed in, only slightly hampered by the bars on the windows. A small table had been set in the sun-path, with a view out to the garden, the grilled front gate, the bluff road, and St. Louis ugly in the distance beyond. On the table was a breakfast service for two.

A dozen dresses were stacked on the big divan before the fireplace. Hatboxes and shoeboxes and luggage were beside it. There was a heap of other packages, captivating in shape and size. No one was in the room Toni crossed slowly to the divan and cautiously lifted one of the dresses. As her fingers caressed the rich dimly remembered texture of rustling silk, a chuckle sounded behind her. She turned. Duval had entered the room. He was fully dressed and she saw traces of fresh mud on the sole-rims of his boots. She dropped the dress.

"They say a woman is not predictable," Duval said "They lie. A woman is the most predictable phenomenon in nature."

"You're sure?" Toni asked.

"Utterly. A dress—some slippers—a few couturier's boxes and the least of them—or the most lethal—is wholly enchanted."

He came down across the room, indicating the dress she had dropped.

"Go ahead," he went on. "They are yours. All them. The best I could find in my warehouses in you size. Nothing finer to be had between here and New Orleans."

She looked again at the dresses. Duval was being modest. There were no finer materials in New Orleans, either. At least not in the New Orleans she remembered.

59

"You must expect a great deal of me," Toni said.

"Do well what I want done in Santa Fe and you will dress in this fashion the rest of your life," Duval answered.

A maid came in, bearing a tray, and went about service at the table with quiet efficiency. Duval took Toni's arm and steered her to her seat. A dewy rose lay across her silver. Duval took his own seat and picked up he flower as the maid continued her service. He turned the rose in his hands, eyeing it appreciatively, until the servant finished and departed, closing the door behind her. Then he handed the flower to Toni.

"A symbol," he said.

"A symbol of what?"

Duval shrugged.

"It makes little difference. A woman always requires a symbol. Some men also, but always a woman. This is yours. Consider it a moment. It is very red, you see. It could be the color of love. It could be the color of blood. It could represent the flame of violence."

"Which is it?"

"That, my dear, is for you to choose when you reach Santa Fe."

"I think you had better speak more plainly," Toni said.

Duval shook his head.

"No. Instructions I might give you could well be less satisfactory than the product of your own unfettered talents. You are a woman and you possess admirable armament. I prefer to leave method up to you."

"Method of what?"

"Certainly that is obvious enough, isn't it? You are to guarantee my full control of the trade centering at Santa Fe."

"Control? That's impossible! There must be hundreds in the trade—maybe thousands."

Duval's smile widened.

"There is opposition, of course. From our buckskin visitor of last night, for instance. From others. I hardly think, however, that they run into thousands. And you will not be entirely alone. I have a man in Santa Fe now. His name is Luis Sebastian. You will work with him. And I will ask no questions when your work is done."

Toni thought of the tall man in buckskin whose gun she had seized. As out of place as he had been in this room in last night's firelight, he had managed to enter the house and leave it again. And he had secured the aid of Tommie Defoe. No ordinary man could have done either of these things. Such opposition, even though it were only one man, might be very troublesome. Duval seemed to understand her thought.

"I do not ask the impossible. I only ask that you do what Sebastian cannot—perhaps only because he is not a woman. Luis is clever. He will be of real assistance to you. And perhaps your task will even be pleasant. I understand Santa Fe can be most kind and generous to those whom she accepts."

Toni thought again of Jim King and the man whom she had shot.

"Did you find them this morning?" Our callers of last night? No."

"They took to the river?"

Duval shook his head.

"No. The grass. They have already started for Santa Fe. It has become very important that Luis Sebastian have your help, Mrs. Palliard."

Toni looked across at the dresses and the boxes. In them lay something toward which she had been striving

61

with almost hopeless bitterness—in them lay a new identity and a new horizon. Not that she felt any lessening of the hatred which had brought her here. Since she now knew the direction of Duval's ambition, she realized she could destroy him more effectively in Santa Fe than she could here. She smiled across the table at him.

"You remind me a great deal of my late husband, M. Duval," she said. "If André Palliard had a fault, it was that he always let his breakfast get cold."

CHAPTER 7

GLORIETTA PASS

THERE WERE TWELVE BIG FREIGHT WAGONS IN THEIR string. Wagons loaded with a fortune in trade goods. Especially two which were loaded to the lashings with powder and firearms, the two greatest treasures Indians could secure. And they traveled without escort—working drivers and wranglers and *cargadores* making up their full force. Toni considered the risk. They had been warned the Comanches were out in force when they left the Arkansas. But still they had turned south without apparent concern. When they passed the second burial ground, so new the graves had not sunk or resodded, she spoke to George Mohler, the train captain.

Mohler was a big, domineering Prussian who handled his freighters with hard-knuckled, ungloved hands. Early in the crossing he had attempted to handle Toni in the same manner, ignoring the widowhood Duval had proposed as a protection for her. There was a certain appeal to the captain's hairy-chested surety and it seemed to give him confidence with a woman. Toni had been obliged to deal sharply with him and he had never fully recovered from his resultant sullenness. He scoffed at her concern over the Comanches.

"Indians! I've got worse worries than them."

"They were enough to stop those burned trains we passed."

"A good wind or a dried up water hole are enough to stop greenhorns."

"But the risk—"

"See here, Mrs. Palliard," Mohler growled, "I didn't get this job by being stupid and I don't hold it by being a fool. It costs two hundred and ten dollars a day to feed the men and animals and meet the charge-offs on these wagons. Save a day in travel time and that's how much money is saved. This Jornada crossing is a good ten days shorter than the Picketwire climb over Raton Pass and maybe a full two weeks shorter than the mountain road in by Taos. That's why we go this way, and your Comanches be damned!"

"How much would you save if the Comanches burned your wagons?" Toni persisted.

"The wagons ain't mine. They belong to Duval—along with everything in them—"

He broke off to shoot Toni a half-knowing, resentful, accusing glance. She understood what he meant. Duval had arranged her passage. Since she had stood Mohler off, she knew the captain had a sneaking suspicion Duval was something more to her than the friend of her dead husband she claimed him to be.

"The Comanches know who this train belongs to as well as I do," Mohler went on. "They'll leave us alone."

Toni was astonished at his surety.

"Does he have the Comanches on his payroll, too?"

63

"Who?"

"M. Duval."

"You taught me to mind my own business, Mrs. Palliard," Mohler said bluntly. "Why don't you mind yours?"

Rebuffed, Toni dropped back to ride abreast of the first wagon. Her questions were unanswered but her uneasiness was abated. As she rode she turned her attention back to the country about her with a growing sense of proprietorship. She felt more than a kinship. It was as though she were crossing a boundary into a land which belonged to her. A land, too, to which she could belong. The limitations which had bound her since Maurice Bandelier's death were falling away like fetters finally dissolving in rust.

Her agreement with Edouard Duval was becoming more than a way to re-equip herself with the dressmaker's and milliner's and bootier's appurtenances she had missed so bitterly since her mother's defection and her father's death—the good living she had once known and to which she believed herself entitled. It was becoming more than a way to secure annuity and independence. It was becoming more, even, than a means to exquisite revenge. It was also becoming a ticket to a new life.

As time went on, Toni could no longer remain back with the wagons, but rode in the advance, brushing stirrup leathers with George Mohler, whether it pleased him or not. Late one afternoon, well into the mountains, she and Mohler turned in advance of the wagons into a small park and saw two men ride from a distant timber patch to hail them. Toni thought the hail was peremptory and glanced at Mohler. He was unperturbed as he gazed at the men jogging unhurriedly toward

64

them. Toni shifted her glance to them and immediately caught her breath. One of the two was Tommie Defoe, slouched gracefully in his saddle with his slender rifle balanced before him. The other was the tall man who had forced his way into Duval's house with Defoe.

Toni knew Tommie Defoe. She knew him even better than he knew her. She focused her attention on Jim King, wary and uneasy. If Tommie had talked of her to his companion, there was already an end to Duval's plans and her own dreaming. As he came up, Toni continued to appraise King carefully. He was like hundreds of others she had seen on the streets and in the taverns of St. Louis and the lower river towns. He was like at least a part of the bull-skinners in the wagons behind her. He favored leather instead of cloth in clothing for the minimum of replacement and repair it required. He was the kind who drove the stock and turned the wheels and skinned the pelts, shedding the sweat involved in most of the labor west and south of the River.

There was, however, something which set him apart. It might be a sureness. Toni didn't know. But because she was watching closely for some sign that Tommie Defoe had talked, she thought the something was in his eyes. They were a blued gray in color. Toni thought they might be angry. Here again she wasn't sure. Eyes could tell a woman about a man when there was nothing else by which she could go. But not with this man. With him the eyes told her nothing. She did not like him for that.

The two approaching men pulled up twenty feet from Mohler and Toni. Defoe looked at Toni, then shifted his rifle and lifted his hat with a mocking smile which yet had a touch of warmth in it. Perhaps as much warmth as he was capable of feeling. She knew then that he had said nothing to his companion. What lay between them

65

belonged only to the two of them still. She eased in her saddle and faced King with a sudden return of confidence. He was not looking at her at all, but at George Mohler.

"Is this string carrying goods to Luis Sebastian in Santa Fe?" he asked.

Mohler nodded warily.

Jim King shifted in his saddle, casually indicating his companion with his thumb.

"This is Tommie Defoe. Came along to keep books for me. To sort of be sure my business is done right. I'm Jim King."

Mohler looked uneasily from one to the other and wet his lips.

"Heard of you. Defoe, too. What's on your mind?"

"Business," King said pleasantly.

"You've sure as hell got none with me!" Mohler protested.

"Unfortunately, yes," King contradicted. "Trade's getting complicated in Santa Fe. Competition, Sebastian calls it. Some of his men turned my store. Now he doesn't want to talk damages because I'm a little short on proof he hired it done."

"What's that to me?"

"Not much, I guess," King shrugged amiably. "You see, we've got law and government on the plaza now. Without proof, I'm sort of stuck, like Sebastian figured I'd be. So now I've got to stick him. Two wagons out of your string—stock, wheels, and loads—ought to just about cover what he owes me."

Mohler glanced at both men and his jaw tightened.

"These are Duval wagons. Just the freight belongs to Sebastian."

"Sort of a question of which pocket you take it out of,

isn't it?" Jim King asked.

"I work for Duval and Company," Mohler said stubbornly. "Sebastian's troubles aren't mine."

Jim King shrugged.

"You're talking about big snakes and little ones, and who can tell the difference between them after you've been bit? I don't know you, but I'll give you the benefit of the doubt. If it'll make you feel better and save your hide with your boss, I'll return the wagons to you in Santa Fe—empty and with my thanks."

Mohler looked down at the wagons now winding up through the park toward them. Toni could feel the pressure building within the man. She recognized as easily as he the bland coolness of this outright robbery—a second attempt at that which had failed at Duval's house in St. Louis.

Mohler finally faced King with an obvious effort at rationality.

"You can't do this. I've got twelve wagons—a full crew. They won't hold still—"

King's amiable smile remained unchanged.

"And there's two of us—me and Tommie Defoe. You make trouble and your boys'll hold still all right— permanently!"

"It doesn't get you any place," Mohler persisted. "It just buys you more trouble than any one man can use. I should think you'd had enough already."

"Of my own, maybe yes," King agreed. "But this has got beyond me and Sebastian—or Ed Duval, wherever he fits in. This is the whole damned territory."

King's eyes flicked for the first time to Toni.

"Your pardon for the truth, ma'am," he added.

Then he turned back to Mohler.

"The outfit you work for just isn't big enough to whip

everybody in New Mexico. It's time it started finding that out!"

Mohler rocked a moment longer in indecision, then he shrugged.

"All right. Pick out the two wagons you want. But go easy on my boys. They'll sit tight. When the string gets up here, I'll have the two rigs you want cut out."

"Including drivers," King prompted.

"Including drivers," Mohler conceded.

King nodded approval.

"You might live a long time," he told the train captain.

Suddenly King's head swung toward Toni.

"Who's this?"

"Mrs. Palliard," Mohler said—a little malice toward Toni creeping into his voice. "Mrs. André Palliard. Another consignment for Sebastian. According to my orders, at least."

King surveyed Toni from head to toe, showing neither displeasure or approval.

"Kind of a perishable item for trail shipment," he said. "Not that Sebastian won't know what to do with it, once he gets his hands on it. But it looks like better merchandise than he generally handles."

"Looks ain't everything," Mohler said sourly.

"They sure help," Jim King countered.

He nodded to Tommie Defoe and they rode down toward the approaching wagons. Toni turned on Mohler in a quiet fury.

"You certainly protect your freight!" she snapped.

"Within risks."

"Risks! Two men against a whole train of wagons. Why, if that Jim King had decided I was going with the two wagons he's stealing from you, I believe you'd

68

have let him take me!"

"I sure would," Mohler agreed.

Toni's fury surged up in her eyes. The train captain made a hasty addition.

"I'd have to. The judgment of God isn't surer than Tommie Defoe's rifle. He could back yonder into the timber and pick half of us off while we were ducking for cover. Just figure you're lucky that this Jim King isn't Sebastian's kind of man. If he was, he'd have taken you, all right."

Toni said nothing to this. The freight wagons approached, flanked by King and Defoe. They singled out two rigs to Mohler. At a gesture from the captain, the two wagons rolled from the line. With a start Toni recognized one of them and spurred over to where Mohler had joined King and Defoe.

"My luggage is in that wagon!"

King removed his hat.

"We wouldn't want to inconvenience a lady by separating her from her pretties," he said. "You're welcome to come with us, Mrs. Palliard. We should be in Santa Fe late tomorrow."

Toni was tempted for a moment. Then she saw Tommie Defoe laughing at her.

"Thank you," she said acidly to King. "Thank you very much. But no."

"We'll leave your luggage for you at La Fonda," King said with a shrug.

Then he suddenly smiled.

"I'm sorry, Mrs. Palliard. I would have enjoyed your company."

He replaced his hat and nodded, dismissing her.

"Tell Sebastian we're even now," he said to Mohler. "Tell him he'd better leave it that way."

69

Mohler made no answer. King gestured to the driver of the first wagon. The man shouted at his team and the two wagons cut from Mohler's string creaked protestingly on toward Glorietta Pass. King and Tommie Defoe reined in behind them. Toni watched their departure with speculation.

These were Duval's enemies in Santa Fe—two of them, at least. Jim King, in particular. A dangerous man, direct enough to have come all the way to St. Louis to solve a problem and resourceful enough to have found a solution here when St. Louis failed him. And he seemed committed to trading even. He should know better. If he didn't, he'd have to learn soon enough. She was working for Duval, and Duval would scorn an even trade in anything. She began to smile a little. A very small smile. George Mohler saw it and swore.

"You got to help me make Sebastian see I had to do this," he said. "You got to help me make him see I had no choice."

Toni nodded, not thinking of Mohler at all.

"Of course," she said. "Of course."

She was still smiling when Mohler started the string and they rolled on in the track of the two stolen wagons.

CHAPTER 8

WETZEL'S OFFER

FRONTENAC PACED ACROSS THE PARLOR OF THE *palacio* like a bee-stung grizzly, growling ominously deep in his throat. Against the far wall he turned angrily back and addressed the room.

"The trouble with this country is there's too damned

many women in it," he said. "Just too damned many!"

"Shut up, Fronnie," Monk Mooney said in earnest reproof. "These ain't women, they're ladies."

Kincaid glanced at Carlita Bent, then at the newcomer beside her—the girl who had been traveling with George Mohler's string of wagons—the widow who called herself Toni Palliard. Kincaid was susceptible to charm, but it was evident what he thought at the moment.

"Carlita is, anyways," he said.

"Women," Frontenac corrected dourly. "Both of 'em. Ladies ain't stubborn an' unreasonable."

Mrs. Bent looked unhappily at Jim King in appeal.

"What can I do?" she asked. "Charlie's up at Taos with Ceran, looking after some business at the store up there. I guess if anybody's in charge here, I am."

"Do?" Frontenac exploded. "Ma'am, that's what we been tryin' to tell you! Jim figured on shippin' these here two wagons he collected from Sebastian up to Taos. Ceran an' Charlie can take the goods in 'em off Jim's hands for a price, an' we'll all get back what we Jim's in furs in Jim's fire. Ain't nothing simpler than that."

"If you start those wagons north, Luis Sebastian will have them trailed," Mrs. Bent said.

Jim made no answer.

"Won't he, Jim?" she asked.

"He might," Jim agreed.

"Won't do him no good, though," Frontenac promised.

"I know," Carlita Bent agreed. "But if he tried to take them back it would mean a fight—more trouble."

"He's been spoilin' for it, ma'am," Kincaid said. "About time we obliged."

Mrs. Bent shook her head impatiently.

"It isn't only that. If you did get those goods through to Taos, Jim, Charlie and Ceran couldn't buy that freight from you."

"Why not?" Mooney asked. "They need all the stock they can get for their store."

"I know. But the Governor of the Territory and his partner can't deal in stolen goods."

"I didn't steal those wagons," Jim said quietly. "I collected them for what's due me. There's a difference."

"To you, of course. But not legally. Charlie can't be party to that."

"But if Charlie and St. Vrain don't buy those goods, how's Jim goin' to pay back what he owes us for them lost furs?" Frontenac asked aggrievedly. "Thunderation, ma'am, even St. Vrain's got somethin' comin' from Jim!"

Carlita Bent spread her hands helplessly.

"I don't know what Jim's going to do, Fronnie—or the rest of you either. But Mrs. Palliard, here, has verified Sebastian's report the wagons were stolen. I can't let Jim take them north. Matter of fact, if I knew where you had them hidden right now, I'd have to send men out to bring them in. You're all going to have to wait till Charlie gets back and can hear both sides."

For the first time since Jim and his companions arrived, Toni Palliard spoke.

"Am I to understand that you are taking no action against these men, Mrs. Bent?"

The governor's wife looked levelly at her.

"Unfortunately, I am not the governor," she said. "I am a wife. And I learned long ago, my dear, to leave the affairs of men in men's hands. I am afraid you will have to wait with Mr. King for Governor Bent's return."

72

Jim rose and took Mrs. Bent's hand.

"I'm sorry to have saddled you with this, Carlita," he said. "You're probably right in what you have to do. I could skin Charlie and St. Vrain for being out of town when I need them."

He headed for the door. The others disconsolately followed him. Fronnie stopped truculently before Mrs. Palliard.

"A word of advice, ma'am," he said. "Mrs. Bent, here, don't know much about liars. They's a bit scarce in this country an' she's shy on experience with 'em. But her husband's an old hand at tradin'. He can spot a liar a mile off. You'd better tell him the perzact truth—just as you seen it out there on Glorietta—about how an' why Jim took them wagons off of Mohler. An' without no embroidery like you give Carlita here."

Mrs. Palliard coolly eyed them all.

"Apparently gentlemen are scarce out here, too," she said. "I wonder if the behavior of the lot of you wouldn't improve if you were all behind bars for a while. That's where you all will be if those wagons aren't returned tonight. I promise you that!"

Frowning, Carlita Bent called after Jim.

"Jim—I'm afraid Mrs. Palliard is right," she said anxiously. "You'd better return them before Charlie gets back. You know how determined he is that none of us offend the law or the people here in these troubled times."

"I'm afraid Charlie has his troubles and I have mine, and we'll each have to whip 'em in our own way, Carlita."

"Charlie is capable of awfully direct action, Jim."

"So am I, if I'm driven far enough."

"It could mean jail."

"Not for anybody in the legion. Charlie knows that. There are some things nobody can do."

Jim pushed the door open and stepped into the darkness of the plaza, followed by the rest. Behind them Jim heard Carlita Bent turn to the niceties of society and the duties of a governor's wife—a task which must often pall on her free and outspoken spirit.

"I'm sorry, Mrs. Palliard, that your first evening in Santa Fe must be spent in this fashion," she was saying. "We do have a more pleasant side. This is quite a good wine from the *palacio* cellar. May I offer you some?"

The others came up to Jim in the shadows of the veranda.

"We told 'em," Fronnie said with pleasure, clouting Jim solidly on the shoulder. "That's what women need—to be told!"

Monk Mooney snorted.

"Listen to the expert!" he said. "You an' women—no wonder you can't even get along with a Ute squaw, thinkin' talk's what they need!"

Kincaid had moved down the veranda a little way. He suddenly stepped into a window embrasure and backed out, dragging a huddled and protesting figure. He signaled Jim, who moved with Mooney and Frontenac down to join him.

"Look what I found," Kincaid said savagely. "Listenin' at the window!"

He straightened the man he held with a sharp, contemptuous jerk. Jim recognized Saul Wetzel's uneasy face. The little trader was openly fearful. He looked swiftly from one face to another, seeming to cringe at the dour dislike apparent in the mountain men.

"I—I got to talk to you, Jim," he quavered.

"You sure do," Jim agreed grimly.

74

Wetzel started to say something, then broke off as the *palacio* door opened behind them, shooting a beam of light into the plaza. Toni Palliard came out, waving farewell to Carlita Bent in the doorway. A wheel grated on stone across the square and a man clucked to a horse. Jim pressed Wetzel and his own companions into the shadow of the wall of the palace. A two-wheeled cart, somewhat similar to half a coach and the only approach to a carriage in Santa Fe, rolled out of the darkness and pulled up before Mrs. Palliard. Luis Sebastian dismounted and helped the girl up to the seat. When she was settled, Sebastian climbed back up and they drove off. Jim scowled after them.

"They're in cahoots," Mooney said with the conviction of instinct.

"Maybe," Jim agreed.

He turned his attention back to Wetzel.

"Start talking," he invited.

"Not here, Jim!" the little trader protested. "In private."

Frontenac shook his head.

"Go easy, Jim," he warned.

"I intend to," Jim agreed.

"You can see this here critter's stripes without no moon," Fronnie said. "You'll be wastin' your time or puttin' your nose into a bear trap."

"I been trying to get hold of you ever since I heard you were back in town," Wetzel pleaded. "Honest, Jim—it's important."

Fronnie leered at the little man.

"Damn!" he growled. "I don't mind toads an' lizards an' such varmints, but it sure does rile me when they rear up an' start walkin' an' talkin' like humans!"

"Leave him be, Fronnie," Jim said.

75

Fronnie stepped reluctantly back and Kincaid loosed his hold on Wetzel's collar.

Wetzel turned earnestly to King.

"Please, Jim—it's very important."

"Now's as good a time as any other," Jim said.

He turned then to his companions.

"Go on back to the wagons. Defoe may get lonesome and this town is full of pretty girls. I'll be along directly. But be careful how you go. Sebastian would give his shirt to know where those wagons are hidden and he'll have every *paisano* in town on the lookout."

"Ever see a time a *paisano* could track a mountain man?" Kincaid asked aggrievedly. "But you ought to come along, too. A man should stick to his friends."

Jim looked at Wetzel. A strange thought crossed his mind.

"Sure," he agreed. "But sometimes the trick is to know who they are. Monk, you know the Portola place?"

"Who don't?"

"Go by that way and see if you can get hold of the old man's daughter. Tell her I'd like to see her."

"That's all you need is to get old Portola mixed up in this!" Mooney protested.

"I said the old man's daughter."

Fronnie shook his head worriedly.

"Ain't one gal already snarled the whole thing up enough for you that you got to have another?" he asked.

"Mind your own business, Fronnie. The Portola girl will understand. She owes me something."

Monk shrugged and angled out across the plaza. Fronnie watched him go with satisfaction, then nudged Kincaid.

"Let's light for them wagons. One of them drivers of

76

Mohler's had a bottle. Monk took it off'n him before we let him run high-tailin' to Sebastian. Monk don't think I know where he hid it, but I do."

Kincaid joined in Fronnie's laugh. They linked arms and moved off down the veranda toward the far end of the plaza; Jim turned to Wetzel.

"What's on your mind, Saul?"

"Not here," the trader said nervously. "Come across to my store."

Jim followed the little man across the plaza. Wetzel had three locks on his door, each with a separate key. He was an insufferable time getting them open. Finally he pushed on the door and stepped aside for Jim to enter.

Wetzel led the way back through the dark trade room to an inadequately partitioned corner where he kept his records and his untidy bed. Here he lit a candle. Jim looked about him. This corner was Wetzel's home. To a man who had spent much of his time under the stars and the sun, walled in only by the horizon, the trader's quarters were repressive and appalling. It seemed incredible a man could live in so small and cramped and disordered a space and Jim was sorry he had agreed to come in here out of the openness of the night for their talk.

Wetzel threw a canvas cover over the rumpled bed and gestured toward it. Jim reluctantly sat down.

"Jim," the little trader said, "Sebastian is trying to buy me out."

Jim was startled. This was something he had not expected. Of the three original traders competing with Sebastian in Santa Fe, anyone would assume Wetzel would be the easiest to intimidate and bluff and drive out. For this reason, he seemed the least-likely to be

77

offered an opportunity to sell his holdings out.

"At a fair figure, Saul?"

"Depends on the point of view, I guess," Wetzel said. "He started out by offering me just about what I have inventoried here. Matter of fact, there was a small edge of profit. I think he must have figured about six per cent on the inventory, and added it to the offer."

It still didn't make sense to Jim. Farady had been killed and his store forced from his widow on what all mountain men believed was a spurious note. Jim King had been burned out. But Sebastian offering to *buy* out Saul Wetzel? Something was wrong. Farady was tough and Jim King was tough, but Wetzel was a mouse.

"You should have sold, Saul," Jim said. "You know there isn't a trader in the country can guarantee himself six per cent on his inventory."

Saul nodded.

"Especially in Santa Fe, the way things are now. I know. But with luck and his usual mark-up, a trader can make a hundred per cent on his inventory. That's why I turned Sebastian's first offer down."

"He's made another?"

Wetzel nodded again.

"A new one every day."

"How much has he come up?"

"He hasn't come up. Each day his offer has dropped a thousand dollars. Started out at twenty-eight thousand dollars. Today he's down to twelve thousand."

Jim frowned. Wetzel spread his hands helplessly.

"It looks like in twelve more days Sebastian will offer me nothing for my store."

"I told you that you should have sold."

"No. But what's it mean, Jim—this kind of thing?"

On the surface, Jim knew very well what it meant.

That it was a waste of effort made no difference. The descending scale of the offers and an obvious time-limit on them was a way of pressuring a timid man like Wetzel.

"Why should Sebastian wait to pound your toes until now?" he asked Wetzel. "Why suddenly decide to give you twenty-eight days before the offer runs completely out?"

"I don't know, Jim," Saul said. "I've tried to figure it out. Maybe the time has something to do with it—something to do with other plans of his. Maybe not. It could be that he figured my inventory at twenty-eight thousand dollars, and cutting it a thousand dollars a day would take twenty-eight days. It could be that just as easy as it could be that twelve days from now something is going to happen and he wants my store and my stock in his hands before it does."

"What kind of a something?" Jim asked sharply.

"I told you I don't know. I don't know anything. I told you I'm just guessing and trying to figure it out."

"Look here," Jim said bluntly, "I don't see why it means anything to Sebastian whether you're operating or not, actually. You don't do anything like the business Farady or myself did. And I should think it would be to Sebastian's advantage to have one competitor left in town—particularly one who didn't hurt his own business enough to count."

"I've thought of that. The only thing I've been able to figure is that maybe there's a big shipment of independent goods on their way out. here from St. Louis, and he might want me out of the way so I can't bid on it against him."

"One way to find out," Jim said. "He'll have to show his hand in the open if he can't bluff you with these decreasing offers. Just sit tight and don't be scared."

"Easy to say don't be scared, Jim, but everything scares me. I'm not a brave man and I remember what happened to your place."

"Luis is too smart to try fire again, Saul."

"There are easier ways to do the same thing. You are a dangerous man, with many dangerous friends. He could not easily have you killed. The fire was best for you, But for me—"

Saul shrugged expressively.

"—I am not dangerous and I have no friends. Who would care if I was found with the knife in the back? But I don't want to die."

"If you're that frightened you'd better take what you can get and sell out now," Jim told him.

Wetzel stiffened.

"Sell out at a loss? I'm not that scared! And I am going to stay in business in Santa Fe. That's really what I wanted to talk to you about. I think I can help you, Jim."

Jim's brows went up. He had thought thought the little trader was just looking for commiseration in his own troubles.

"Help me—how?"

"Kincaid was right. I was listening at the *palacio* window. I heard what you were saying to Mrs. Bent. Now that you can't send those two wagons on up to Taos to be sold to the governor and Ceran St. Vrain, what are you going to do with them?"

"I don't know."

"I will buy them from you—if I can get them at a price."

"If you listened well you know Sebastian claims I stole those two wagons from him. He expects to get

80

them back, one way or another. If you get them, he won't like it, Saul."

"I am not in business to keep Luis Sebastian happy."

"Are you prepared to offer cash?" Jim asked sharply.

"No, not cash. I don't have enough. And if I did, I wouldn't dare risk it. But I'll advance you enough to pay off your friends for the furs they lost in your fire. You'll get the rest as I sell off the goods. You can't get rid of them any place else."

"You could just be trying to get them back for Sebastian."

"I'll pay thirty thousand dollars for them over a period of six months. You know Sebastian wouldn't go that far."

"I tapped Mohler's wagon string for a little nuisance and expense money, over what I figure Sebastian owes me, Saul. The freight in those wagons is worth closer to forty thousand."

"I know," Wetzel agreed. "But I'm entitled to a wider profit where the risk is so high."

"Do you ever think of anything but profit?" Jim asked acidly.

"Not often," the little trader admitted. "I am a lonely man. My pleasures are simple and profit is one of them. Do we have a deal?'

Jim nodded.

"Be sure there's nobody else is around your store the rest of the night. If there is—if it looks like a trap—I won't bring the wagons in. Keep your hands high and clean. My friends and I will handle the unloading if it looks all right."

Wetzel smiled.

"I've tricked a few men in my day," he said. "I hope to trick a few more. But you're not one of them, Jim."

He followed Jim to the door. Jim turned to face him there.

"This sure bails me out of a hole, but I hope you know what you're doing, Saul."

Wetzel smiled again, a sad, crooked smile.

"Don't strain yourself, Jim," he said. "You're just like the rest. You really don't care whether I tangle with Sebastian over this or not. You don't care what happens to me, as long as you a get that freight unloaded without trouble and you get paid."

He waved his hand as Jim started to cut in.

"It's all right, Jim. I'll handle Sebastian if I have to—in my own way. And you'll be paid."

CHAPTER 9

CASA PORTOLA

THE WAGONS WERE HIDDEN UNDER A HIGH OVERHANG in the brushy bottoms of Santa Fe Creek, four miles above the town. When Jim returned, the camp was in an uproar. Frontenac had been right. He knew where Mooney had hidden the whisky commandeered from Mohler's driver. And he and Kincaid had knocked it off between them. Monk, coming up from the town with Dolores Portola, had discovered the perfidy. He was understandably angry and Kincaid and Fronnie, with alcoholic wariness, had thought it wise to lash him to a wagon wheel to keep him from getting reckless. The result was volcanic.

In spite of the necessity for quiet and avoidance of discovery of the wagons by Sebastian, Jim could hear Monk's swearing for a quarter of a mile as he approached. And he found Dolores Portola crouched against the other wagon, eyeing Frontenac and Kincaid with uneasy distrust. Angry and impatient, Jim silenced the outraged Mooney with a word and ordered the other two to free him.

Frontenac was scandalized.

"He's a wild man," he protested. "You heard him an' all he aims to do. Would you turn him loose on us—us that have give you the best we've got? They ain't a man in the mountains would do a ornery, inhuman thing like that to his partners. Why, Jim, me an' Kincaid been like brothers to you. It just ain't civilized to toss your brothers to no old curly-tailed wild wolf like that'n!"

"You stole his whisky," Jim said. "Now you can pay for it."

"With our lives?" Kincaid asked aggrievedly.

Jim found another bottle in his own gear and crammed it into the caterwauling Mooney's pocket. His two companions promptly freed Mooney and the three of them started in on this new supply. The dispute was settled. Jim then approached Dolores Portola.

"I'm sorry, señorita," he said wearily. "Mountain men are always best in the mountains. They get sort of restless around a town."

The girl eyed the three veterans of the leather legion.

"Restless?"

She shivered. Jim grinned.

"Well, thirsty, then."

"Drunk!" she corrected.

"Not really," Jim said. "You ought to see them when they are."

"No thanks!"

Jim dragged a camp box around for a seat and the girl sank onto it.

"You sent for me. Why?"

Jim pointed to the wagons.

"I have to turn those and what's in them into money. I thought you might help me find buyers among your people. But it won't be necessary now."

"You've found a buyer?"

Jim nodded.

"I'm sorry I couldn't get word to you in time to save you the trip out here."

"*De nada,*" the girl said automatically. "You have made the sale?"

"Say I have made other arrangements than the one I was thinking of when I sent for you."

"It is wrong," the girl said. "Those are Luis Sebastian's wagons."

"They're the thirty-eight thousand dollars he owes me. You remember, I'm sure—"

Dolores Portola looked levelly at him.

"Yes, I remember. That is why I am here."

"I'm grateful you answered my message—"

Jim broke off, suddenly realizing something was missing from the camp.

"Wait a minute—"

Mooney and Frontenac and Kincaid had gone around to the other side of the wagons. He followed them, leaving the girl alone.

"Where's Defoe?" he asked sharply.

"Lit out for town the minute me an' Fronnie got back," Kincaid said.

"What for?"

"Burr under his tail, maybe," Fronnie said.

"What did you idiots let him go for?"

"Didn't see no point in stoppin' him," Kincaid said innocently. "It left more whisky for Fronnie an' me."

"Didn't he say where he was going, what he was going to do?"

"You know it ain't fittin' to ask a man about his private affairs like that, Jim," Fronnie said severely.

He waved the whisky bottle.

"An' you ought to be able to lay your hands on better drinkin' pizen than this!"

"Give it back if you don't like it," Jim suggested.

Frontenac raised the bottle to his lips, and, keeping a limpid eye on Jim, drained it dry. Then he flung the bottle at Jim's feet.

"Not that I was complainin', mind you," he added.

"Listen," Jim said sharply, "I want the three of you to span up the wagons and bring them into town on the old creek road. I doubt Sebastian figures we'll come right in with them, so you stand a good chance of getting by. Turn into the alley behind Wetzel's place. But one of you go ahead of the wagons. If there's a sign of anybody but Saul, double back and bring them back here if you can. If it's all clear, I'll meet you behind Saul's store in an hour."

"An hour," Fronnie said carefully.

"We'll be there, Jim," Mooney agreed.

"See that you are!"

Jim doubled back around the wagons to where Dolores Portola was waiting.

"I'll walk you back to town, señorita."

"No, if you don't mind," she said. "My father would not approve—my brothers. And it would get to them if I was seen with you. There was enough risk, sneaking out of the house when guests were expected."

"Wouldn't approve?"

Jim was surprised. He had not been an intimate of old man Portola or his sons, but he had considered them

85

friends—as good friends as he, had among the old families of Santa Fe.

"What's the matter with me of a sudden?" he asked. "I've done a lot of business with your father and your brothers. They know me well."

"Of course, señor. But you are *yanqui*."

"I'm New Mexican—as New Mexican as they are!"

"They would not agree—not by several generations—not by several hundred years. It is best I go back alone."

Jim shrugged. Still irritated by his friends' drunken spree, he was in no mood to argue with the girl. The old families of Santa Fe had many strange convictions, and when a Yankee encountered one of these, it was almost a hopeless task to argue it away. The girl hesitated before turning away, then spoke swiftly and so softly he could barely understand her.

"There are many meetings in Santa Fe these days. There is much talk in secret. I do not know what it means, but I think it is not good for *yanquis*. You are much hated."

She hurried away then down the bank of the creek. Jim scowled after her. She was out of sight in the brush before he came to the conclusion that what she had said meant nothing unless he knew what she was driving at. He should have questioned her. Seeing that Mooney and Frontenac and Kincaid were already bringing up the wagon stock, he also started down the creek.

Jim approached the Portola house silently, trailing Dolores by a few yards. To avoid startling her he had intended to accost her as she reached the haven of her doorway, but he saw this was impossible. Quite surprisingly, for the lateness of the hot hour, the windows were brightly lighted and the hum of many voices hung over the invisible courtyard. He remembered Dolores had said guests were expected, but this was an unusually large gathering and more were an arriving.

Two young men, whom Jim recognized as Archuletas—scions of another powerful local family—rode up to the main gate and were admitted, still mounted, into the courtyard. Jim noted that Dolores, still ahead of him, flattened against the wall of the house to avoid being seen by the newcomers as they approached. When they vanished through the gate she moved on again.

Jim picked up his own pace, hoping he could catch the girl's attention, but at the same instant a figure stepped from an angle of the wall and blocked the girl's way. The figure was Luis Sebastian. Jim halted abruptly, pleased to discover he had closed the gap between the girl and himself sufficiently to hear what was said.

"Your father and your brothers have looked all over for you," Sebastian said sharply. "Where have you been?"

"For a walk."

"Tonight—of all nights! Where—with whom?"

"To a blind witch's house with a drunken Indian for company," the girl answered contemptuously.

Sebastian moved like an angry snake. The slap of his hand against the girl's cheek carried clearly to Jim.

"You little fool, this is no time for joking! Get inside!"

Sebastian thrust the girl roughly along the wall to a small, recessed door, and they vanished into the house. Jim slid on along the wall, vanishing into the same recess as two more riders came clattering along the road and up to the main gate. As his swung open to admit them, they were momentarily flooded with light and he stiffened in astonishment.

The woman was the young widow who had argued against him in Luis Sebastian's behalf before Carlita Bent—the Toni Palliard who had come out to Santa Fe on George Mohler's Duval wagon train—the baggage Mohler had implied was assigned to Sebastian personally. Her companion was Tommie Defoe.

Encountering them elsewhere in the town, Jim would have thought little more of their being together than a touch of envy at Tommie's easy gallantry and swift success with women. But he was thunderstruck at their presence here. Certainly Dolores Portola had been trying to warn him when she spoke of the meetings being held in Santa Fe. It was a warning he judged to be more important than his own battle with Sebastian. Now he wasn't so sure.

Had the guest list at the Portola house been limited to those of Spanish name and descent, he would have thought it had some political importance. But not the recently arrived widow from St. Louis. And above all, not Tommie Defoe. These were outlanders—outlanders of questionable background besides. Of all the *yanquis* in Santa Fe, these two were the least likely to be accepted in a gathering of the people of the old time.

And there was another thing. The acquaintance between the Palliard girl and Tommie Defoe was no casual thing achieved since their arrival. An unmistakable intimacy between them had been obvious—something which could not have been fabricated in a single hour together.

For several moments Jim remained motionless in the recess after Defoe and Toni Palliard had been admitted to the Portola house. His mind went back to the night in St. Louis when Tommie Defoe had declared himself in on the visit to Duval's house on the bluff. The little man then had said he wanted money. And since he had made none on the long crossing to Santa Fe, he must still want it. Money could have brought him here tonight. For money he could have arranged to be a guest of the Portolas'. But whose money, and how was it to be made?

Jim swore silently to himself. It was hard when a man became accustomed to the unswerving loyalty of such comrades as Frontenac and Kincaid and Mooney—the stout friendship of St. Vrain and Charlie Bent and the others who made up the buckskin legion—to understand that there were those whose personal profit and benefit measured ahead of friendship. There would be no trouble making Defoe talk once Jim could get his hands on him. Men in the mountains learned the tricks of this, too. And separated from his deadly little rifle, Defoe was not formidable. The difference in size between Jim King and himself would automatically ensure a reasonable attitude on Tommie's part.

But Toni Palliard was another matter. The Portolas were beyond doubt the proudest and most haughty family in Santa Fe. They were an old family and their tradition was old and they possessed a full measure of the shrewd caution inherent in their Spanish blood. They were most unlikely to take up with newcomers from the States for many reasons, including a possible introduction by Sebastian, whom they persisted in regarding as their own kind. When a newcomer was an unattached woman of unknown background as well as a *yanqui,* her admittance to the Portola house was as astonishing as was Defoe's.

Jim fitted it carefully together. That both Defoe and the Palliard girl had been invited here—or at least accepted—indicated each had something for which those within were willing to overlook deep-rooted tradition and normal custom. Jim's personal interests and his nature forced him to view Santa Fe and anything that happened within the town from a trader's point of view, and he could not help remembering Toni Palliard had brought letters of introduction into New Mexico. Therefore she knew someone of influence in St. Louis—someone of sufficient influence to put her aboard a string of Duval wagons in the beginning.

The apparent closeness of Defoe and the young widow was not so complex as he ran over it again in his mind. It could be that quick kinship which springs from a common desire for money. It could also, he realized, be something much older, springing out of the past. What was important to Jim now was that if Defoe and the widow were making alliances in Santa Fe, they were making them on the wrong side of the fence.

For several minutes Jim considered knocking on the courtyard gate of the Portola house and trying to gain an entrance. But he knew that if his intrusion was not resisted with force, it certainly would be resented, and with the mood the town was in, further resentment would gain a *yanqui* nothing. Charlie Bent was right in this. The Yankees of Santa Fe had a grave responsibility in these first few months of rule by the States to avoid giving the old blood of the town provocation upon which real trouble could be based.

He turned at last toward the plaza with the taste of disappointment strong in his mouth. Even then he could not decide whether this was because of Tommie Defoe or the Palliard girl. He had come to count on Defoe's help in breaking the trade monopoly Sebastian and Duval were trying to establish, and he had become attached to the dapper little man. His apparent defection stung. But Jim knew he had also become intrigued by Toni Palliard, and whether this was the time to admit it or not, he was distressed that she had apparently joined an opposing camp.

Lantern light glowed through the back door of Wetzel's store. The wagons were drawn up in its shine. Laden silhouettes were passing through the doorway. Whatever the nature of the party or meeting at the Portola house, it was keeping those who might otherwise have been interested in this business off the streets.

Frontenac, sweaty and dusty from shouldering boxes and barrels, emerged from the door as Jim came up.

"Saul said we ought to get the unloadin' done in a hurry, so we started," he said. "All right?"

Jim nodded. Fronnie scowled at him.

"Smart one, ain't you?" he complained. "Riggin' it so we do the unloadin' while you gallivant. Where work is, that's where Jim King ain't. That's how you can tell he's boss."

"Me—boss?" Jim grinned. "Never thought I'd hear you admit that!"

"Slip of the tongue," Fronnie growled. "You sure this deal you made with Wetzel's honest?"

"Honest enough. Why?"

"He's hurried us so fast we ain't even had a chance to catch our breath. Look here, Jim, you wouldn't involve good honest friends like us in somethin' dishonest, would you?"

"Not unless there was profit in it."

91

"I knowed we could trust you," Fronnie said sourly. "Ol' Jim King—straiter-laced than an old maid's corset! The wagons is about unloaded. What you want done with them?"

"Drive them around to the plaza where Sebastian and the rest of the town can find them in the morning. Outspan the teams and turn them loose. Where's Saul?"

Frontenac gestured inside. Jim entered the store. Wetzel had driven himself a good bargain. Goods from the wagons were stacked almost to the ceiling in one corner and Saul was taking a hasty inventory. When he saw Jim he ducked into his corner quarters and came out with a buckskin bag.

"Enough to pay for the furs your friends lost in the fire," he said.

Jim hefted the bag. It was heavy with coin.

"A little expense money for you, too," Saul added. "The rest in six months. That was our bargain?"

Jim nodded.

"Then get out of here," Saul said nervously. "Go away, so's I can lock up. I don't want to make too much of this. The streets have been quiet and I don't want to press my luck. Get out of here with your friends—out of town is best—before you're seen and it's all over Santa Fe that you were here."

"You're not going to be able to keep this from Sebastian, no matter how hard you try."

"No. But I don't have to wave it in his face either."

"Good luck," Jim said.

He lifted the buckskin bag again and went back out into the alley. Frontenac and the others had already rolled the wagons away. He met them coming back from the plaza afoot, and he gave the buckskin bag to Kincaid.

"This takes care of the furs you boys lost with me. Everybody's share is there, including St. Vrain's and a bit of my own. The Colonel'd better take care of it till the rest of you are ready to split it into grubstakes, for next season. I want you to take it up to him at Taos."

"Wasn't you supposed to give Defoe some back wages from the first money you got in, Jim?" Mooney asked.

"I'm not keeping any for myself. Defoe can wait, too."

"Sure," Mooney agreed. "But will he? He sure likes pocket music."

"He'll like it better when he's got the gold to clink."

Mooney shrugged and was silent. Kincaid frowned thoughtfully.

"St. Vrain's apt to have gone over to his place at Mora by now, Jim," he pointed out. "He don't usually stay very long at Taos—specially when Charlie Bent's up there to look after the store, too."

"Then go by Mora on your way north."

"Anything you want me to tell St. Vrain—or Charlie, if I see him?"

Jim shook his head.

"Just hunches. Reckon they'll keep."

"Maybe I better wait around a couple days and see if anything comes out in the open," Kincaid suggested.

"You're not waiting an hour," Jim said firmly. "That money's got to get out of Santa Fe tonight. We can't take a chance on Wetzel getting scared of his bargain and changing his mind. And when Sebastian finds out exactly what we've done with his wagons, he isn't going to sit still."

Kincaid nodded agreeably.

"Don't worry about the money," he said. "I'll be in

Mora tomorrow night and Taos the day after."

Jim nodded approval and shook Kincaid's hand. Things were quiet enough. If something broke into the open—if he needed St. Vrain and Charlie Bent, they were only two days away. Kincaid moved off into the shadows with the long, shuffling reach of a mountain man with a journey ahead of him. Jim turned to Frontenac and Mooney.

"If I don't show up in the morning, you two drop by and see Mrs. Palliard. Ask her where I am and make her tell you. She'll know."

"Kind of late to be callin' on ladies, ain't it, Jim?" Frontenac asked disapprovingly.

"Looks like my business, from where I stand."

"Old Charlie said we was to keep our nails clean," Mooney cautioned righteously.

"I can't afford to wait," I Jim said. "Hope I haven't waited too long."

"I never figgered you for the impatient type," Fronnie said. "I'll tell you somethin', boy—the longer you wait, the sweeter they are. Seasons 'em. Like peaches. Gives 'em time to ripe up."

"I don't like it," Mooney said.

Fronnie snorted at him and clapped a big hand to Jim's shoulder.

"Don't mind old wet-nose. I'm kind of glad to see you headin' for a little fun. You been livin' too serious since you got back from St. Louie. All I ask is you takes your boots off like a gentleman."

"You're drunk again," Jim observed with some accuracy.

Fronnie was outraged.

"Both of you," Jim added with conviction.

"Me and Monk, drunk, on the same bottle? An'

94

havin' to share it with Kincaid, too? Jim, you got a mistrustful nature!"

Fronnie linked arms with Mooney and they stalked off. Jim watched them head off toward the camp on Santa Fe Creek, then he turned across town toward Toni Palliard's house.

CHAPTER 10

MIDNIGHT CALL

TONI PALLIARD'S HOUSE WAS DARK AS JIM WALKED toward it and he altered his original plan of waiting outside for the return of the young widow from the Portola house. He had no idea how communicative Toni Palliard would be when he faced her, and there was much to be learned about a person from a study of the surroundings in which they lived. He judged he would have ample time to learn about Toni Palliard before she returned.

A shutter responded readily to the blade of his knife. Although the window was small, according to the custom of this sun-drenched and too brilliant country, he was able to lift himself through it. Standing on the floor inside, he drew the shutter closed again and faced the darkened room.

Remaining completely immobile for a long moment, he made certain he was alone in the house. This was automatic, rather than a studied caution. It was a strange thing, but wholly true, that in the solitude of the mountains a man learned to sense the immediate presence of any other living thing when there was neither sound, scent, nor sight to go by.

Moving carefully along the wall, Jim came to a sideboard and found a candle in a candleholder. Opening his jacket, he lighted the candle in the shelter of the buckskin. By keeping his body turned away from exterior windows, he thought he could move through the house with sufficient light for his is purpose and little chance that the illumination would attract attention or even be visible from the outside.

The house was scrupulously neat and orderly. The furnishings were those available in Santa Fe at a modest price. The luxuries of toiletries and personal clothing discovered were not as numerous or extravagant as he expected. As a matter of fact, there was nothing which could not have been purchased across the counter of the Duval & Co. store in town. The whole house was characterized by modesty and economy and a very simple order of femininity. Jim was frankly surprised.

There were no letters, no mementos, no memoirs. It appeared Toni Palliard had left her former life completely behind when her husband died—or at least when she set out for Santa Fe. Jim was disappointed in this. He hoped some clue of family or friend would throw a little light on the owner of the house. But Toni Palliard and her reasons for coming to Santa Fe remained as much of a mystery as before.

Jim made a very careful search. A man accustomed to the subleties of the trails was not a apt to overlook significant detail. Consequently, the candle burned low before Jim was finished and he reckoned he had been in the house nearly two hours when he heard hoofbeats outside. He extinguished the candle and swiftly returned to the room by which he had entered the house.

Two figures rode up to the gate at the foot of the path leading up to the house. One was Toni Palliard.

However, the other was not—as Jim had anticipated it would be—Tommie Defoe. The man was too tall, a little too heavy, and he recognized Luis Sebastian. The man dismounted and helped the girl alight. He spoke earnestly with her for a while, apparently urging something which met with little favor. Abandoning this finally, Sebastian gave the girl a package, took the reins of the girl's horse, remounted his own animal, and rode off.

The girl came through the gate and started up the path toward the house. Jim glanced at the window by which he had entered. There was time to leave as he had come, and he meant to delay facing Toni Palliard until he could learn a little more about her. But there was something troubling him. Suddenly he knew what it was. There was something familiar about the package Sebastian had handed the girl. On this, Jim changed his mind. He groped for a chair, sank into it, and waited.

Toni Palliard came in through the door in the darkness with much rasping and clattering of a key in a lock with which she was not yet wholly familiar. She fumbled a bit, putting down the package she had carried up from the gate. It clinked dully. Jim's lips compressed. She moved then to the sideboard and felt about there for the candleholder Jim had used. He had not replaced it, and she stood motionless for a minute before turning and feeling her way back through the house toward the kitchen.

He could hear her kindling another candle there. While she was gone from the room, he crossed quickly to the package that she had put down on a stand near the door. He needed no light to identify it. His fingers told him all he needed to know. She had brought home with her the buckskin bag full of coin that Saul Wetzel had given him in payment for the two wagonloads of freight he had sold the little trader.

Knowing Kincaid, Jim was sure the money could not have changed hands except by violence, and he cursed himself for exposing Kincaid to this. He cursed himself for not realizing Sebastian could not be as easily tricked as he imagined. Obviously the Duval manager had known where the wagons were from the time of their arrival in the camp on Santa Fe Creek. When Toni Palliard's intercession with Carlita Bent had failed to have them officially seized, Sebastian had kept Jim and his companions under close watch. It was like Sebastian to permit Jim's deal to go ahead, content to take Jim's profit out of the deal he made and leave settlement with Wetzel till later.

Jim stepped back to the chair and waited for Toni Palliard to re-enter the room. However, she did not come directly back into the front of the house. Instead, she went along a back hall to the bedroom Jim had searched so thoroughly. Humming to herself, she moved around in there for a little while. Finally, a connecting door opened and she came into the room where Jim waited, bringing the light with her.

There was a long moment in which she did not see Jim and he stared at her. She was dressed for bed.

Her nightgown was no filmy affair, translucent and clinging, but a soft, full-cut flannel, more apt to be comfortable in the night chill of Santa Fe's altitude. A pair of soft, flaring, ankle-topped squaw Indian boots were on her feet. Her hair had been brushed and now hung at her back. The flannel lay soft against the upper part of her body and along the line of her thighs and she was very beautiful. Jim tried hard to remember, but he thought he had never seen such beauty except the night he had stolen into Edouard Duval's house in Santa Fe and had seen the hooded dancer named La Fleur.

Toni Palliard caught her breath and froze motionless when she saw Jim. He rose slowly from his chair and took off his hat for the first time since he had entered the house. She put down the candle and glanced wildly about the room for an instant as though for something to cover herself. Then realizing the impracticality of this—or that it was already too late—she lowered her crossed, shielding hands and arms and looked levelly, almost challengingly at him. He had an instant's knowledge that she knew her beauty and was proud of it—that she would use it as she could—that there was no real distress for her in standing here before him like this.

He had dropped the buckskin bag of coins to the floor beside his chair. He kicked it.

"Where did you get this?"

"You must have been standing here, looking out. You must have seen him give it to me."

"Who?"

"Luis."

"Sebastian?"

"Yes."

"Where did he get it?"

Jim's voice was steady, flat—harsh.

"Ask him," the girl said.

Jim gave no warning he was going to move. Suddenly he had stepped forward, seizing her arm, and her eyes widened.

"I'm asking you!" he snapped.

The widened eyes closed again so that the lids half veiled them. The stiffness went out of the arm he held. Jim retained the grip a moment longer until she smiled mockingly at him, then he freed her. Now she, in her turn, casually prodded the buckskin bag on the floor with her toe.

"We have more than that to talk about," she said.

She moved across the room and stopped by a divan.

"I was hardly expecting you, Mr. King, but since you are here—"

She sank onto the divan. Jim did not like the feeling of being left standing alone, so he sat down, resentfully.

"Luis has told me a great deal about you," Toni Palliard said. "George Mohler, too, after you took those wagons away from us in Glorietta Pass. Your friend Mrs. Bent spoke of you at length before she sent for you when I made my complaint to her. And it even seems to me I heard some talk in St. Louis before I left. Jim King—free trader."

"That about sums it up, all right," Jim agreed bluntly.

"I don't understand you then. Trade is for profit, isn't it?"

Jim nodded noncommittally.

"Then why can't you take your profit when it's offered to you? Why do you have to fight for it?"

"Where's Kincaid?" Jim said.

"Somewhere in town, I understand, nursing a broken head. Probably he's with your other friends by now. Luis's men were gentle. Luis only wanted your money—not your friend's life."

"Luis!" Jim spat the name out. "Mohler tried to tell me you were Sebastian's woman."

"Mohler has a jealous disposition and a nasty mind," Toni Palliard said easily. "I'm nobody's woman. It just happens that I have an interest in Luis Sebastian's store."

"Sebastian's store belongs to Duval and Company."

"I know. In a way, I suppose I'm Mr. Duval's

partner—in a very small way. He has been very generous to me."

She paused thoughtfully, studying Jim.

"I think he would be to you, too, if you'd give him a chance. You could be a partner, too. You could have a house of your own out here on the hill instead of having to break into one belonging to someone else. You seem to make a habit of breaking into houses."

"Defoe told you about the call we made on Ed Duval in St. Louis, then."

"Yes. I forgot about Tommie, didn't I? Well, he's told me a lot about Jim King, too. If I believed all I've heard, I think I'd have to be afraid of you."

"But you're not."

"No. And there's no need for you to be afraid of me."

"How long have you known Tommie Defoe?"

The girl pursed her lips thoughtfully.

"I don't suppose I really do know him, even now."

"I saw you with him at the Portolas'."

"So that's why you came here—to catch us together if you could."

"No. I came to see you."

The girl looked at him and laughed.

"Then for heaven's sake, be civilized about it!"

"I'm trying to be."

"Sneaking into the house—spying— Tell me what you want. I'll be as helpful as I can."

"I haven't any reason to believe that."

"Well—" Toni Palliard laughed again. "I do have to protect my own interests."

Jim knew she was baiting him. He also knew that his greatest danger was in responding to her—man to woman. He rose easily, crossed the room, and sank down beside her, much closer than the width of the divan demanded.

"This is a lonely country, isn't it?" Toni Palliard said.

"For some," Jim admitted.

"You are the first man who has been in this house at night alone with me."

She leaned back. It angered Jim that she knew what he would do, but he could feel her warmth and the faint, sweet women scent of her body and his arms went around her, drawing her against him as he found her lips.

He meant it to be simply a masculine thing, but he was electrified with a compulsion he had never known before. He freed her quickly, with an intense and wary feeling of having been shaken to his roots. He saw astonishment in her eyes and a kind of wonder. She straightened, then rose and paced quickly down the room and back. Halting beside the chair where he had been sitting, she bent and picked up the buckskin bag filled with Wetzel's money. Crossing with it, she dropped it on the divan beside him.

"This is legally Sebastian's," she said. "Take it. I can promise you the rest Wetzel agreed to pay you, too."

Jim shook his head.

"It isn't enough. I had to make a short deal with Wetzel—considerably short of the thirty-eight thousand dollars Sebastian owes me."

"All right, then," Toni Palliard said impatiently. "Enough more to make up the thirty-eight thousand dollars. Enough to set up a new trading post any place you want in the mountain country north of here. I'll make Luis agree somehow. Only you have to get out of Santa Fe. And all of your friends with you. And you won't come back—any of you."

She saw Jim stiffen.

"At least this season—"

Jim started to shake his head.

"Not for a month, at least—" she amended.

Jim thought of the strange, decreasing offer Sebastian had made Wetzel for the purchase of his store—an offer that would take a month to shrink from its initial figure to nothing. He thought of the meeting at the Portola house and the other meetings Dolores Portola had mentioned.

"Why a month—why just a month?"

"No questions," Toni Palliard said sharply. "Give me your promise and take your money."

Jim rose, shaking his head.

"I'm taking the money. It's mine. But no promise. Tell Sebastian to leave Wetzel alone—to keep out of our way. We want free trade in Santa Fe and we're going to see we have it."

"You're very sure."

"I am—very."

"You're a fool!"

"No," Jim said. "But somebody else is. We stick together. Sebastian should know that. Kincaid never did like Sebastian. He isn't going to have any use for him at all after tonight. The rest of us, too—Frontenac and Mooney and St. Vrain—even Governor Bent, when the chips are down. Luis has gone as far as he can go. Tell him that."

Toni Palliard gripped his arm with apparent earnestness.

"You've got to understand," she said. "You must leave Santa Fe. All of you. Stubbornness means real trouble—even for Governor Bent, if he isn't reasonable. I'm trying to warn you, Jim!"

"I've been warned a couple of times before," Jim

answered dryly. "But I've managed to stay around."

"Talk to Tommie Defoe, then. Tell him I told you to. Maybe he can make you see you've got to get out of Santa Fe."

Jim picked up the bag of money.

"You can bet I'm going to talk to Tommie," he said. "But it's him that's going to get the warning—not me."

He crossed to the door, slid back the latch, and pulled it open. The girl followed, and when he stepped out on the little entrance veranda, she came with him. A night breeze, lifting from the town, pressed her gown against her.

"I'm serious about this warning," she said. "I've planned too long a time. I won't change my plan. And I can't warn you again."

"I suppose in common courtesy I ought to thank you for it, then," Jim said dryly. "That what you want?"

He started to turn away. She caught him and flung her body against him and kissed him again, then ran back into the house, closing the door and dropping the latch behind her. Jim went slowly down the path to the gate and turned toward the up-creek brush where his camp lay.

Jim walked slowly, reappraising the past hour. Disturbing as she was, and perhaps dangerous, Jim had learned something from Toni Palliard. Not fact, perhaps, but conviction. And a mountain man often survived by what he sensed rather than what he knew. The young widow had a connection with Duval—perhaps through her dead husband, as she claimed, perhaps through some other channel. And she had been sent to Santa Fe, or had come here of her own will, to do just what she had tried to do tonight—to persuade Jim King and others of the buckskin legion to leave the territorial capital.

She had specified a month—a time element he knew she had not intended to reveal. Jim believed that Duval or Sebastian—perhaps both, one upon the orders of the other—hoped in thirty days or less to seize the whole of the Santa Fe trade. Knowing his friends, the men who had made that trade, Jim knew this could not come about except by violence. And suddenly what had been a personal matter between himself and Sebastian—or himself and Duval—had now become a larger quarrel embracing the territory itself.

Were it not for this conviction, Jim knew he could not have left the widow's house. He would have stayed. And as it was, he knew he would be tortured through many solitary hours when his mind turned back to this night. He would remember softness and warmth and how Toni Palliard had looked, standing before him with a candle in her hand and her hair falling down her back and her body dressed for bed.

CHAPTER 11

HOSTAGES

MOONEY AND FRONTENAC WERE IN THEIR BLANKETS when Jim arrived at the camp on Santa Fe Creek. Kincaid lay between them, mouth open in a snore and blood caked in his hair from a bad scalp wound over one ear. Jim grinned in spite of himself. Kincaid's report of the attack on him and the loss of Wetzel's gold would have made Mooney and Frontenac as furious as the injured man himself. But because Jim King was absent and the three of them looked to him for direction, they had rolled into their blankets to sleep while they awaited his return.

Beyond the embers of a fire, Tommie Defoe was hunched on a grounded saddle, staring at the ebbing coals. He remained unaware when Jim materialized soundlessly out of the darkness and started only when Jim's moccasins entered his range of vision beside the fire. But his nerves were iron enough, for he only looked up even then, and remained where he was as Jim crossed toward the sleepers.

Jim bent above Kincaid and slipped the retrieved bag of money in beside the injured sleeper where he would find it when he woke up. Then he turned back toward Defoe. Tommie silently rose as though on signal, and preceded Jim into the night, away from the others. He continued far enough so the sound of their voices would not rouse the sleeping men, then turned to face Jim with an apologetic but guarded defiance.

"That the money they took from Kincaid?" he asked.

Jim nodded.

"How'd you know about that?" he asked Defoe.

"How'd *you* get it back?"

Jim looked levelly at the little man.

"From Toni Palliard," he said.

"Then you listened to her!"

Defoe's relief was obvious. It darkened as Jim shook his head.

"No. I just took the money."

"Sebastian was with her. You took it in front of him?"

"He didn't come in the house when he brought her home. I was inside, waiting."

Defoe's eyes appraised Jim in silence.

"You took her to Portola's, Tommie. Why didn't you bring her home?"

"Sebastian wanted the pleasure," Defoe said. "In

106

Santa Fe, everybody does what Sebastian wants."

"Including you?"

Defoe hunkered down at the base of a tree.

"Look, Jim, face it," he said earnestly. "I'm not spilling anything, since you apparently saw me going to that meeting—or least know that I was there. Sebastian has all the old families in town behind him. Portolas—Archuletas—I don't know how many more I met. A lot of them, though. Probably all of them. And all with him. You don't stand a chance, trying to buck the whole town."

"That's my decision, Tommie—not yours."

"If they want to give all their trade to Duval and Company, you can't stop them. Why should you try? It's their town. Let them do what they want with it. Get out of Santa Fe—while you can."

"You changing horses, Tommie?"

"Maybe."

"Is there real money—the kind you've always wanted—in switching like this?"

"I'm not switching and I'm not doing it for money—I'm just throwing in my cards in a game where I know I can't win. You ought to have the sense to do the same." Jim studied Defoe for a long moment in speculation and appraisal, then struck suddenly, without warning.

"I kissed that widow a little while ago. She kissed me. I could have stayed all night."

Defoe's face instantly drained of color, although not one muscle of his body moved. He spoke slowly, quietly, with a great effort at levelness.

"I'm glad you didn't."

"Why?"

"Glad for you."

Jim hunkered down beside the little man.

"Maybe you'd like to tell me who Toni Palliard really is—what there is between you."

Defoe lifted his head.

"Yes, I would, Jim. More than you could guess. It would clear up so much. But I can't."

"Why?"

"That's something that doesn't concern you. Leave it alone. Just don't let anything happen to her—anything at all!"

There was sudden whiplash forcefulness in this last. Jim rose again to his feet.

"Keep her out of my way if that's the way you feel," he growled. "I've got enough rocks in my moccasins, already!"

Jim tossed a couple of sticks of wood on the fire for light and prodded the sleeping Frontenac with his toe.

"Indians!" he hissed.

Fronnie and Monk and Kincaid came up out of their blankets, clawing up their weapons with a deadly, automatic precision. They looked wildly around, the glance of each coming at last into accusing focus on Jim. And their resentment was not lessened by Kincaid's discovery of the bag of money. Jim looked off into the darkness toward the place where he had been talking to Tommie Defoe. He wanted the little man to hear what he had to say. But Defoe had not followed him back to the fire.

"What's eatin' you, Jim—turnin' us out like this?" Fronnie growled.

"There's too much ticking going on and I'm tired of trying to guess what it means.'

Fronnie tipped his head alertly.

"Ticking?" he repeated. "I don't hear anything."

"If you had this lump on your head you would,"

Kincaid growled. "Right inside your own skull. There's whispers afoot all over town. That what you mean, Jim?"

Jim nodded.

"More than whispers, too. Hunches. Things happening without reason. Things shifting around too fast to keep track of them. Ticking covers it."

"A clock don't tick if it ain't running , that's for sure," Kincaid said.

Jim nodded again.

"And it can't run if it gets taken apart. Besides, the best way to find out what makes something go is to look at the pieces it's made of."

Fronnie brightened.

"I busted a trade watch open once," he said. "Just for the hell of it. All sorts of the damnedest things inside!"

"You're getting the idea, Fronnie," Jim told him.

Mooney was getting the idea, too.

"Sebastian first," he proposed eagerly.

"Yeah," Kincaid agreed. "And them *paisano* thugs he set on me. He's the mainspring. Get him first."

"Maybe he's the mainspring and maybe not," Jim corrected. "We'll leave him be and watch him for a spell. Kind of work around him on the little pieces. They're apt to tell us more than in he ever would."

The other three looked at one another, measuring the proposal. A grin ran from one to the other.

"Put some coffee on, Monk," Kincaid said. "Let's hear the rest of what Jim's got on his mind."

Jim and Frontenac separated from Kincaid and Mooney at the corral behind La Fonda. There were already lights up in the hotel kitchen where breakfast cooks were at work, but Jim thought there was enough time before daylight at least to get started, if he and his companions moved fast enough.

Rummaging in a debris pile near the smithy flanking the hotel corral, he found a two-foot section of rusty brake iron which he judged a substantial enough bar for his purpose. He gave it to Frontenac and led the way past the side of the hotel to angle directly across the plaza toward Wetzel's door. As they moved he searched the plaza for Mooney and Kincaid, but apparently they had already made their crossing and were off on their own errand.

Wetzel's three locks were tightly in place. Jim lifted his improvised bar and fitted it into the hasps of the locks, then relinquished the iron to Fronnie. The big man tested the bite and purchase of the bar, then hunched his massive shoulders with apparent effortlessness. Tortured steel and rending wood shrieked loudly for an instant—an alarming sound in the predawn quiet. But it was over so quickly Jim thought it could not be identified by startled listeners, if there were such, unless it was repeated. And repetition was not necessary. All three of Wetzel's locks and their hasps dangled uselessly.

Jim pushed the door open and quickly stepped inside. Frontenac stepped in behind him and as the door closed each automatically stepped aside from the portal, freezing in his tracks. There was utter silence for a moment. Then, off to the rear, where Wetzel's sleeping corner was, a gun sear clicked softly as the weapon was carefully cocked. Jim heard no other movement, but Fronnie was suddenly close enough to grip his arm delightedly. Then both moved, separating, weaving through the invisible maze of counters and aisles to converge from two sides on the sound of the cocking

110

gun.

It was tense and troubling work, with only instinctive sense to warn of unseen obstacles. And always there was the knowledge that a man as habitually fearful as Wetzel would almost certainly fire at the first inadvertent sound. Marksmanship without light was impossible, particularly at the hands of a man as unfamiliar with guns as the little trader, but there were such things as luck and chance and who could figure the odds under such circumstances?

Measuring his progress carefully, Jim thought he was a scant yard away from the corner where Wetzel had his miserable and untidy quarters, when there was a grunt of suddenly and forcefully expelled breath and a brief, violent struggle which eased swiftly into silence. Frontenac whispered almost in Jim's ear.

"Got him. Now what?"

"This way," Jim said.

He worked cautiously into Wetzel's sleeping place. Frontenac followed him. Jim drew partitioning blankets tight and lit a candle. Fronnie held Wetzel's entire face clamped in one huge hand, effectively silencing him. The other hand held one of Wetzel's arms in the small of his back, enforcing instant obedience.

"Kill him if he tries an alarm," Jim whispered, more for Wetzel's benefit than Fronnie's. "But turn him loose."

Fronnie obeyed. Wetzel flexed his clamped jaws and glared angrily at Frontenac before facing Jim.

"What's the idea?" he whispered, unsteady and careful to avoid offensive truculence.

"Something's going on in Santa Fe, Saul," Jim answered. "In the alleys and behind closed doors. More than Sebastian just sniping at me—at us. We want to find out just how much more you know about it than we do."

"Persecution!" Wetzel squeaked bitterly. "I try to be your friend and you persecute me!"

"Yep," Frontenac said. "That's a fact. And I kind of enjoy it, too. Now—you going to talk?"

Wetzel turned back to Jim in fresh alarm.

"You going to let this—this animal handle me?" he begged. "And after the way I bought you out of your trouble tonight?"

"Neither one of us know about trouble yet," Jim said. "I turned your money over to Kincaid and started him out to Taos or Mora to find St. Vrain. He didn't even get out of town before some of Sebastian's thugs took it from him. How'd he know Kincaid had it—that I had it? Maybe you can answer that, Saul."

Wetzel's eyes widened in what Jim reluctantly recognized as genuine surprise. But before the little man could answer, the street door of Wetzel's store swung open and footfalls entered. Jim thrust the candle under Wetzel's bed, where overhanging blankets would shield it, and Frontenac again clamped the little trader in helpless restraint.

"Who's there?" Jim challenged.

"Me an' Monk," Kincaid's voice answered. "We caught one of our birds keepin' watch at the other end of the plaza. Didn't have to go to his house at all. How about some light?"

Jim retrieved the candle and pushed back one of the curtains. Kincaid and Mooney dragged another man into Wetzel's now crowded quarters. He was disheveled, a little dazed, and as frightened as Wetzel himself. Jim saw with satisfaction that he was the younger of the two Archuleta brothers who had earlier ridden into the

Portola courtyard.

Actually, he wanted both brothers, but maybe it was lucky Mooney and Kincaid hadn't taken any more time. It was already dangerously close to full dawn. And if men from the Portola meeting had been posted as night guards in the alleys of Santa Fe, their surveillance would be even more thorough in daylight.

Jim nodded for Fronnie to free Wetzel again, and he spoke bluntly to their new prisoner.

"I don't suppose there's any point in warning you. You know more about the game we're playing than we do. And you know just how dangerous bucking us is going to be."

"What do you want?"

"Just exactly who was at that meeting tonight—what was it held for—what does Luis Sebastian expect to get out of it?"

Young Archuleta set his jaw.

"Get that from Sebastian," he said. "You won't get it from me, you *yanqui* pigs!"

Mooney clucked his tongue in malevolent sympathy.

"Strong words, sonny. Wonder if your brother'll talk the same way when we've got him and he's got to stand and watch what we do to you?"

Archuleta paled perceptibly. Then he stiffened.

"But you don't have Juan."

"Give us time," Mooney said affably. "We just got started. You an' Wetzel in twenty minutes. Not bad, eh? We'll get brother Juan all right."

Archuleta's eyes shifted to Wetzel.

"What's he's got to do with it?" he asked sharply.

"We'll find that out, too," Frontenac promised.

"Jim—Jim, listen to me—" Wetzel pleaded.

Kincaid had been looking out through the blankets

113

and across the store to the street. He scowled at Jim.

"Gettin' light, fast. We got to get 'em out of here in a hurry if we're goin' to hold 'em without being seen."

Mooney scowled also.

"Where can we take 'em? Got to be some place where they won't be found. And there's others we got to rope in, too."

Jim nodded. He wished Charlie Bent were in town. He was sure Charlie would give his plan a try, once he understood it. He was sure Charlie would let him use the sanctuary of the *palacio* and the security of the old prison rooms in the government house. But Charlie was in Taos and Carlita had made it plain the stand she believed she had to take. He knew that he didn't stand a chance of persuading Carlita Bent there was a shred of evidence or logic in what he was doing. She was too determined to defend Yankee justice in her absent husband's name.

Saul Wetzel was still tugging at Jim's arm.

"You got to listen," he insisted. "What do I have to do to make you see that I'm with you in fighting Sebastian the best way I can? I gave you money, Jim—does it have to be blood? Or my right hand, maybe? You want a place to hide Archuleta—any others you may take? I got a cellar under the store here. I never use it. I bet there aren't three men in Santa Fe ever knew it was here, and they've all forgotten it."

"No good," Jim said. "The minute you show up missing, the first place Sebastian will take over will be this store. And he'll search it from top to bottom to make sure it's all his."

"Sure—if I show up missing," Wetzel agreed anxiously. "But why do I have to do that? What if I'm around—open for business as usual—what then?

Nothing. Not for a few days, anyhow. Not as long as Sebastian keeps making me those decreasing offers— not until he starts doing something else. Nobody'll find out."

Jim appraised Wetzel slowly and very carefully. The hiding place Saul was suggesting was even better for his purposes than the prison rooms of the *palacio*. But because it was ideal, it could be a well-baited trap if Wetzel so chose. And the trader was not one of the legion. A man could not accept him as such.

"I may be making a mistake," Jim said slowly. "If I am, it's likely my last one, Said. But it'll be yours, too. How do we get into this cellar?"

Fronnie and Mooney and Kincaid stared in astonished disapproval at Jim. Wetzel shouldered them aside and dragged his bed around to reveal an old trap set in the floor beneath it. The hole into which the ringbolt of the trap was set and the crevices around the door itself were filled with dirt. It had not been opened for a long time. At least Wetzel had not lied about that.

Fronnie bent and put his back to the lift. The trap gave protestingly. As it came up Jim handed Archuleta a candle and pushed him onto the ladder leading into the musty darkness below. Archuleta halted when his body was half below the floor. He glared up at Wetzel.

"I'll report this at the next meeting, you miserable, money-grabbing *yanqui*-lover!"

Jim put his foot on the top of Archuleta's head and pushed down hard. Archuleta descended into the cellar. Kincaid seemed to understand. He followed. Mooney reluctantly did likewise. Only Frontenac balked.

"You crazy, Jim. We'll be worse off down there than mushrats in a gang-trap!"

"If we all disappear with Archuleta, it's going to

make it just that much harder for his friends to figure out what's happened to him. And the more they worry, the more careless they're apt to be, Fronnie."

"Worry!" Fronnie snorted. "Ain't none of 'em'd worry like I would if I was down in that hole. No, sir, Jim, I hanker fer air and sky and good smellin' and you don't get me down there!"

Wetzel shot Jim a shrewd look.

"One thing, Jim," he said. "There's two casks of Spanish wine down there. Very old wine, very potent and very valuable. Please leave those casks alone, hunh?"

Fronnie was tempted and showed it, but in the end he shook his head stubbornly and started to turn away. Jim thrust out a foot, seized one of the big man's arms, and jerked him off balance. Fronnie took a backward step and vanished down the trap with a stentorian bellow and a great wheeling of arms and legs.

CHAPTER 12

WETZEL'S FORT

THERE WERE TWO CASKS IN WETZEL'S CELLAR, ALL right, but they did not hold any rare old Spanish wine. They proved to contain the liquid fire of ordinary Taos Lightnin', from Turley's Mill at Arroyo Hondo. Fronnie was so furious at Jim's trick of dumping him into the cellar that it is doubtful wine would have sufficiently mellowed him to get over his grudge. But the Taos Lightnin' succeeded admirably. Once Fronnie surged up the ladder to the trap door which Wetzel had lowered over them and put his head to the underside with such

116

force that the ladder creaked ominously.

But bolts had been shot above and even the big man's immense strength could not budge the trap.

When he came back down the ladder he glared at Jim, but did not voice his accusation. Instead, he crossed over to young Archulteta and jerked him to his feet.

"So you like Sebastian, eh?" Fronnie growled. "So you like whistlin' through the grass like a snake on its belly, schemin' against honest men like Jim, here—an' us—and Ceran St. Vrain an' Charlie Bent!"

One of the big man's palms smacked against the side of Archuleta's head, slamming him to the floor. Mooney and Kincaid scooped Archuleta up and thrust him back within Fronnie's reach. This was not Jim's way, but he did not interfere. Frontenac and Mooney and Kincaid were his kind. If their ways were not always his, they had the same right to secure the information Archuleta possessed as he did. And this was no longer merely money and profit and trade. It was no longer the fierce pride and resistance of men of the mountains to encroachment of freedoms and opportunity. It was something more vicious.

Fronnie did not strike the young New Mexican again. Instead, he seized the collar of Archuleta's expensive jacket and shook him bodily until his head cleared.

"So you want only Duval and Company trade in your miserable mud town!" Fronnie snarled. "Company trade—no independents. You sniveling young pup, you got any idea what the difference between a company and free traders like us—like Jim King—is? Well, I'll tell you! It's the difference between bein' a slave an' a free man. You an' your stupid, stiff-backed friends are weldin' on your own shackles! All we're tryin' for is a chance to save you from the rope you're knottin' about

117

your own necks. Tell us what Sebastian is up to an' we'll keep him from doin' it—as much for you in the long run as for us. An' so help me, that's a fact!"

"I'll tell you nothing!" Archuleta said defiantly.

Jim admired the youngster's courage in the face of Fronnie's threats. They said in the mountains, with more truth than fancy, that a rutting grizzly had been known to turn tail on Fronnie when he was in a rage.

Fronnie spun Archuleta away from him with a snort of disgust and turned on Jim.

"We're nailed down here like so many corpses in a coffin," he growled. "What we goin' to do?"

Jim shrugged.

"I don't know about the rest of you," he said quietly. "But I'm about as short on sleep as I like to get and I don't know when it's going to be this quiet again. Reckon I'll try catching up while I've got the time."

While the others, including Archuleta, stared, Jim made himself comfortable with the aid of some old sacking. His companions were still staring in sullen disapproval when he puffed out the single candle and plunged Wetzel's cellar into darkness.

Jim was not certain of the hour, but he judged it to be well into the morning, when he was awakened by heavy footsteps overhead. There seemed to be a great many more feet and considerably more activity than Wetzel's usual morning trade would justify. The traffic and movement continued for a few minutes, then subsided and finally died out altogether. His companions, rousing one by one during the peak of the commotion, looked to him for explanation. He kept them signaled to silence until there was silence above. Even then he had no answer to their questions. When Archuleta, glaring truculently at his captors, made his own hopeful guess,

118

Jim let it stand.

"My friends," the young New Mexican said with relish, "taking care of Wetzel. Take care of him very thoroughly, it sounded like. The good God knows he's had it coming long enough. They'll presently get to the rest of you, too."

Fronnie shook a huge balled fist under Archuleta's nose.

"Try invitin' 'em down here," he suggested. "You'll find out what a good taking care of really is. Go ahead—just open your mouth and see how fast I stopper it for you!"

Archuleta shook his head and sank back down and was quiet.

The day dragged slowly, most of it in complete darkness, for Wetzel had not been generous with the supply of candles with which he had sent them into the cellar. They all began to be uncomfortable with thirst and the raw whisky in the casks did nothing to alleviate this, although all of them tried it in varying quantities.

Once Archuleta, without provocation beyond the unspoken thoughts in his own head , burst into sound, swearing at length in bitter Spanish over Yankees in general. Jim tried to draw him out on the basis of this hatred, but succeeded in flushing out only one furious statement.

"You're fools—all of you! Maybe you can fight Edouard Duval and Luis Sebastian, but you can't fight New Mexico!"

The distress which struck the youngster as soon as these words were out of his mouth was so obvious that Jim realized the New Mexican believed he revealed more than he wished. Yet it was not in fact a revelation at all. Jim considered it carefully and came to the

119

conclusion that Archuleta—in his scorn of them as aliens—did not realize they understood the general Mexican hostility to Yankees here.

Sunset came and went somewhere above the unchanging darkness in which they restlessly idled. Night chill began to permeate even the cellar. The store overhead, which had been ominously quiet throughout the afternoon, now became utterly still and remained so. Restlessness continued to build in Jim until he could abide it no longer. He took a candle stub and examined the underside of the trap at the head of the ladder, determining how it was hung upon its hinges.

The pins were mortised into the floor above, but there was a bit of rot in the old timber, and Jim thought that with patience and a bit of blade work with a stout knife, it might be possible to work them free through the fit of the trap. It was better than sitting motionless below, and they might be able to give their jailer a nasty surprise if Wetzel continued to make no move to free them. Or if the knife did not work, there was another way. Since they had not been disarmed, they had considerable powder upon them. Carefully planted, it would take the trap out with a flourish. Jim leaned to this more spectacular method.

Climbing back down to his companions, Jim started to suggest his plan to them. He was interrupted by the sudden sliding of Wetzel's bed overhead. The bolts of the trap rattled. Jim snuffed the candle he bore. Fronnie grabbed Archuleta's arm in so sharp a warning that the young New Mexican gasped with pain. And they all waited tensely.

The trap slowly creaked up after a moment, but no light came from above. The trap slowly lowered again, and a man felt his way down the ladder. At the bottom he halted, fumbled about, and sparked a candle alight.

Even Archuleta stared incredulously. The man was Saul Wetzel, all right, but he was hardly recognizable. He had been methodically and brutally beaten. He was rocking a little on his feet. He had obviously looked to his own injuries to the best of his ability, but his breathing was ragged still, and he could speak only with great difficulty.

"The broken locks on the door—Sebastian saw them," he said. "He was sure you had been here. He was sure I knew where you were—where Señor Archuleta was. It took him an hour to decide I didn't know. And his best men worked on me. Didn't you hear them this morning?"

Jim thought of the traffic overhead—what they had thought to be only an unusual amount of trade. For that hour Wetzel had been fighting for them. Not with them, but for them—and alone. And without an outcry. Had he shouted, this also would have been audible through the floor, along with the scuffling boots of his tormentors. And had his shouts been heard in the cellar, Jim knew he and his companions might have attempted to force their way from what they thought was their prison, but which was actually their hiding place. Had they done so, they would have betrayed themselves.

Saul had known this, too, and he had kept silent. Jim King knew violence and he knew what this effort had cost the little trader. The brutality of his punishment and torture was plainly written on his battered face.

"I'm afraid we made a mistake about you, Saul," Jim said slowly. "I'm sorry."

"Yeah," Fronnie agreed, head hanging in self-condemnation. "A hell of a mistake! I'm sorry, too. We all are."

"Forget it," Wetzel said. "We put up with what we

have to. I was brought up to learn that lesson ahead of everything else. Important thing is I convinced them you weren't here—that I didn't know where you were—that I didn't care. They won't be back. Won't even watch my place, I don't think. I waited till now to make sure of that."

"Where do we stand now?" Jim asked—more of himself than of the trader.

"That's up to you, Jim," Wetzel wheezed. "You didn't worry Sebastian much when you were where he could keep track of you. But he's worried now he's lost you. He's worried plenty—"

Wetzel paused, as though intending to say more, but a paroxysm of coughing shook him. He clutched at his side, paled, and collapsed under a wave of pain. Fronnie caught him as he fell and carried him to Jim's improvised couch of sacking. Jim knelt and peeled Wetzel's shirt back. The whole of the little man's torso was livid, with great, ugly contusions welling up beneath the sparse, graying hair covering his chest.

"Ribs broken," Jim said grimly, "Boots. They kicked the hell out of him."

Archuleta bent close, staring with fascinated horror.

"Sebastian did that?" he asked unsteadily. "Just to make him talk?"

"You think maybe he made it up?" Fronnie growled.

Archuleta shook his head dumbly. Jim pulled the injured man's shirt closed.

"Blankets," he said over his shoulder. "From the store. Plenty of them. And some of that whisky."

Fronnie and Mooney lit another candle and climbed the ladder. Kincaid turned toward one of the whisky casks, but Archuleta was ahead of him, filling a tin cup with an unsteady hand.

Jim got a little of the fiery liquid past Wetzel's lips. Frontenac and Mooney came back down the ladder from the store with a double heap of thick trade blankets. They helped Jim wrap Wetzel in them with the curious, soft-handed gentleness of big men stirred to sympathy. Jim watched the little trader anxiously for a few moments. Presently Wetzel's pallor began to lessen a little. Frontenac sucked in a huge, audible breath of relief. Jim rose grimly to face his companions.

"We've got some more visits to pay. But one of us has got to stay here—to look after Saul and keep an eye on our prisoner."

Mooney and Kincaid and Frontenac all nodded agreement, but none of them volunteered. Jim knew how they felt. A similar savagery was pulsing in him. Each wanted the freedom of the night and an opportunity to get his hands on one of the those who had worked Wetzel over. Each knew this was no real way to repay Wetzel for what he had done for them, but for the moment none of them could think of any other coin. And in the back of the mind of each was guilt over the distrust and suspicion with which they had considered Saul while he was in fact lying on his bed above in silent, solitary agony

Young Archuleta solved the problem. His eyes shuttled from one to another of his captors. His head finally dropped.

"I don't suppose you're going to free me."

"You're damned right, we're not!" Fronnie snapped.

"And you can't leave Wetzel alone. You couldn't. So I might as well look after him for you."

Jim was as startled as the others.

He'll be all right," Archuleta said quietly. "I'll take as good care of him as you could till you get back."

Jim and the others still remained incredulously silent. Archuleta raised his head and met their doubtful stares, coloring angrily.

"I'm giving you my word," he said sharply. "Isn't that enough? Or do you think every New Mexican is the kind of beast who would do a thing like that?"

He pointed to Wetzel's figure. Jim eased then, and smiled a little.

"I've got a notion there might be quite a few New Mexicans us bullying Yankees could get to trust and like a lot if we got half a chance," he said. "Come on, boys."

He crossed to the ladder. Monk and Fronnie and Kincaid followed him uneasily. When he looked back into the cellar as he lowered the trap, Archuleta was already bending over Saul, straightening his covering in an attempt to make him more comfortable. He grinned then at his comrades and Fronnie and Kincaid and Mooney eased, doing what he had already done—taking Archuleta at his promised word.

Bolting the trap from above and again covering it with Wetzel's bed, the four of them moved through the dark store and stepped into the night-shrouded plaza through the unlocked front door. They kept to deep shadow in the plaza and cut across to the Street of the Old Ones. In a few moments they were bunched against a wall across the street from Sebastian's house.

Jim studied the opposite building, trying to determine how best to divide his little force. Before he reached a decision, the main street door opened and a knot of a dozen men emerged, standing in a group in the column of light from within. Central in the group were Sebastian and Juan Archuleta, their prisoner's older brother. Both were dressed in high, Spanish riding boots

124

and carried small, tight saddle-rolls under their arms.

Among the others were Old Man Portola and his two sons. Most of the rest Jim thought were Duval & Co. men—or Sebastian men, however was best to say it. Some were from the Santa Fe store Sebastian operated and some were travelers who usually made the rounds to Testuque, San Ildefonso, Pojoaque, and other valley settlements, for the Indian trade to be had there. George Mohler was among them. It was with a strange sense of relief that Jim failed to spot Tommie Defoe in the group.

Hostlers brought two saddled horses around from the rear of the house. They lashed Sebastian's and Juan Archuleta's saddle-rolls onto the cantles of the saddles. These two swung up, waved farewells, and set their spurs. Jim and his companions swore softly as they helplessly watched two of the men they wanted most ride swiftly down the street and turn eastward on the Glorietta Pass road.

Still, something was better than nothing, and since Sebastian and Juan Archuleta were now temporarily out of reach, Jim turned his attention to the three Portolas. They were probably as good a source of information as Juan Archuleta, if all three were taken and played against one another. The trouble was, of course, that there were three of them, and Juan Archuleta's capture would have been a sufficient lever to use against the brother already their prisoner.

Old Man Portola and his two sons started unhurriedly along the street, accompanied by all but one of the Duval & Co. men. George Mohler alone had gone back into Sebastian's house. Jim and his companions followed the Portola group for a little distance, but it was pointless, as it would be impossible to separate the Portolas from so large an escort.

Suddenly an idea struck Jim. It wasn't the best idea he had ever had, but it was the best that came to hand for the moment, and he decided it would have to do. He nudged his companions, signaled them to follow, and then cut across the broken lots to their left at a light, noiseless run, making for the bridge across Santa Fe Creek above the Portola house.

The servant who answered Jim's knock at the service door of the Portola house seemed distraught. She shook her head vigorously when he asked for the Señorita Dolores. The Señorita was not in. Then suddenly the woman caught his arm as though in concession to a concern which overcame her better judgment.

"You come from the town?" she asked anxiously.

Jim nodded.

"You have seen the patrón and the Señorita's brothers?"

Jim nodded again and added that he believed the men of the family were even then on their way home. The servant's agitation instantly become more marked and Jim realized Dolores Portola in fact was absent from the house—that this servant woman knew where she was and was in mortal terror the girl would not return before her father and brothers did.

The woman seemed about to turn dispiritedly back into the house. Then her face suddenly flooded with relief at something beyond Jim. She rushed past him, scolding in imperative, hurrying Spanish, too excited for him to follow its meaning.

Some distance away and near the place Jim had left his three companions, two figures were sauntering toward the house—the missing girl and a man. The servant was running toward them. Knowing how close the Portola men and their escort must be by now, Jim

126

had no choice if his scheme was going to work at all. He signaled his hidden companions and raced forward, overtaking the servant in a dozen strides. In the shadows ahead, in response to his signal, Fronnie and Monk and Kincaid broke cover and swung into motion.

The servant woman cried out in fresh alarm as Jim raced past her. Up ahead, Frontenac's huge figure blanketed Dolores Portola and the man with her. Kincaid and Mooney flanked the mountain giant. Dolores cried out once at their sudden materialization. A gun, high and sharp in report, snapped angrily. An oath sounded. Bodies collided. There was the fleshy sound of swift, efficient blows. Jim reached the struggling group as the Portola girl broke away from Kincaid. Jim seized her and jerked her roughly around.

"Take it easy!" he said savagely. "We're no worse than Sebastian."

The girl twisted, saw his face for the first time, and ceased struggling. The servant darted back toward the house, shrieking alarm at the top of her voice. Down the street, now dangerously close, came the sound of running feet. Jim knew these were the Portola men and the group which had left Sebastian's with them. He saw over his shoulder that Frontenac had hoisted the limp form of Dolores Portola's male companion to his shoulder.

"Circle south and back to the plaza," he whispered to the others. "Stick with me."

Tightly gripping one of the Portola girl's arms, he started off at a ragged run, dragging her with him. Fronnie, with his burden, and Mooney and Kincaid, strung out behind him. They clattered across the creek on the first bridge below Portola's, and recrossed it on the second. A gun snapped twice behind them at the second crossing, but Jim heard at least one of the bullets clip through brush on the wrong side of the stream, and he thought his ruse might be working.

Cutting through the crazy-quilt pattern of old streets in the lower end of town, they turned up no further alarm, and the uproar of pursuit faded behind them. Jim took a chance then, and turned directly toward the plaza in the hope of getting out of sight before Portola's party turned out the entire town. They made it across the open of the square without seeing anyone in the darkness, and they ducked into Wetzel's store.

Kincaid was the last through the doorway, lagging a dozen yards behind the others. Jim waited impatiently for him and slammed the door closed as he came through.

"Getting old?" Jim growled.

"Seems like," Kincaid agreed dourly. "Too damned old for this!"

Mooney had Wetzel's bed kicked out of the way and the trap up. They all scrambled down the ladder and lowered the trap over their heads. As soon as the door was down, Archuleta kindled a light. Frontenac dumped the limp form of Dolores Portola's escort on the blankets beside Saul Wetzel. Jim grunted in astonishment. Fronnie's captive was Tommie Defoe.

CHAPTER 13

THUNDER!

JIM SWUNG TOWARD THE PORTOLA GIRL, WANTING THE truth of Defoe's connection with her family and its friends—with Luis Sebastian and the strong undercurrents of Santa Fe—but he was arrested by a thunder overhead, not in Wetzel's store itself, but in the

128

plaza outside—the pound of many feet. His trap—his hunch—was working. And the rest of it could not be sprung here, underground. He jerked his head at Frontenac and Mooney and Kincaid

"More customers," he said. "Come on."

Kincaid stirred apologetically and stepped away from the foot of the ladder, leaving a pool of blood on the floor.

"Afraid I'm a mite peaked for another chore, Jim," he said reluctantly. "They got lucky and got a bullet into my leg, back there on the creek."

"You could have said something!" Fronnie growled at him with a mountain man's typically masked sympathy.

"We was moving too fast," Kincaid answered. "You go ahead. I'll stay here and keep an eye on the pigeons we got already."

Jim nodded and spoke to Dolores Portola.

"We're going after your father and your brothers. Fix up Kincaid's leg and see if you can help Señor Archuleta with Wetzel."

"You expect a great deal for one favor, Jaime King!" the girl said bitterly.

"I know," Jim agreed. "But I don't have any choice." As he started away, his eyes fell on Defoe's unconscious body.

"Kincaid!" he said sharply. "Watch Tommie when he comes around. He's got a lot of explaining to do and I haven't got time to wait."

The Portola girl's frown deepened but Kincaid nodded and Jim went up the ladder before Dolores could protest further. Mooney and Frontenac were waiting for him in the darkness of Wetzel's store. Candle lanterns were bobbing about in the plaza. It was evident by now that the Portolas had suceeded in turning out a good half of the able-bodied men of their race in Santa Fe. And they obviously intended to comb the town clean.

Two men, passing, paused near the door of the store. One was about to enter when the other stopped him with quick dissuasion in Spanish.

"Nobody there," he said.

"You are sure?"

The other nodded.

"Even the Jew has left since Luis questioned him. They are all hiding in the hills. It must be."

"Señor Portola says no," the first man disagreed. "They have not had the time to get out of the town with the girl. They must be about."

"We won't find them, looking where they are not."

The first man shrugged and the two New Mexicans moved on. Mooney touched Jim's arm in the darkness.

"Notice something funny?" he whispered.

"What?"

"Remember them guns, back at the bridge?"

Jim nodded.

"They had a nasty crack to 'em—like a good trade rifle—not the old bull-roar of the kind of smoothbores they've mostly got in this country. An' look what they're all carryin' out there in the plaza now!"

Jim looked and realized what Mooney meant. Every man in the plaza was armed with a trade rifle of identical make and pattern. New guns, good ones, which could only have come from the unusually large stock carried in Sebastian's Duval & Co. store. The out-dated and ineffective European weapons with which the citizens of Santa Fe usually armed themselves were completely absent. And it was certain in the new rifles had not been issued in the last few minutes, merely to make easier the capture or annihilation of the Yankees who had kidnaped Fernando Portola's daughter. Jim recognized grim significance in this, but it was a thought for later. What was important now was that the plaza was too full of searchers to risk dodging into it from the store.

"The back door," Jim whispered.

Fronnie reached the alley entrance first. Jim would have cautioned him to be quiet, but he was too late. Fronnie batted the bar up and jerked the door open to reveal two dark men outside, alerted by the sound of the bar and waiting with ready guns. Had Fronnie dodged back, as would have been human and normal in a lesser man, each of the pair in the alley would have fired, and at such close range they could not have missed. But tonight battle was a joy in Fronnie's soul. The big man was a great animal on the hunt and he did not pause as the door swung open, but launched himself in an eager flying leap. His sweeping arms caught the two men and bowled them back and over before their startled reflexes could function. He relinquished one to Jim and Mooney and quickly silenced the other with his hands. Mooney gathered up the fallen guns. Fronnie lifted a limp body under each arm.

"Can't leave 'em here," he said, "like a cougar leavin' her kill for the dogs to find."

"The ruins of my store," Jim suggested. "They'll be out of sight there. And it won't mean anything if they're found. Meet me at the end of the alley."

He ran off down the passage then on silent moccasin feet, leaving Mooney and Frontenac to follow when they disposed of their chore.

This end of the alley gave out onto a short street running into the plaza. As Jim emerged from the alley, a

131

man was loping along this street from the square. He hauled up with a sharp Spanish query for identification.

"*Quién es?*"

Jim answered him with a leaping forward stride and a swinging right hand which slammed him against a wall. The man sagged and pitched headlong to the pavement. Jim was forced to flatten against the wall himself as another man ran across the head of the street and halted at sight of the sprawled figure. For a moment the man was motionless in indecision. Then he turned and shouted into the plaza at his back, gesturing impatiently at the same time. With a lift of pleasure Jim recognized him as Feliz Portola, the elder of the old man's two sons. But the pleasure was short-lived.

Others joined young Portola at the head of the street, in answer to his hail. Two men. Then two more. Then another. The six of them charged down in a body toward the body of the man Jim had felled. Caught alone against the wall, Jim braced himself, knowing he could not use his gun without bringing on the whole town and the odds were now too steep for him to face this any other way with any hope of success. When young Portola's party was almost on him and discovery was an instant away, Frontenac and Mooney came charging out of the alley. They tried to halt, thought better of it, and plowed full into the New Mexicans as though they were a flying squad instead of only two men. At the same moment, Jim charged out from the wall, hitting the New Mexicans from the side. They were knotted defensively close together and surprise hampered them.

One swore as Monk grappled him. Jim dropped another with a swipe of his pistol. He rammed the muzzle of the weapon into the back of a third.

"Quiet!" he warned with sibilant sharpness.

The one word was enough. The rest recognized the tautness of the whisper and they all seemed to have a high regard for the safety of the man he covered. None of the six made an outcry and resistance abruptly ceased. The man against the muzzle of Jim's pistol turned a little and Jim saw the arrogant, aristocratic features of old Fernando Portola. His eyes darted to the others, now there was time for identification. One was Real, the old man's other son. Another was Henry Chavez, head of a clan nearly as important as the Portolas. The last man Jim did not know, but he thought the fellow was likely a *paisano* from one of the big households. So he and Mooney and Frontenac had their game—all of it they needed—if they could hold it.

"Pick up behind us," he told Fronnie.

Nodding to Mooney, he started crowding their captives toward the alley. For a moment it seemed they would not go, but the ease with which Frontenac scooped up the limp figures of the two men who were down seemed to impress them. They grudgingly gave ground.

As they passed the gaping door of the fire-gutted building which had once housed Jim's store, Frontenac dumped his limp double burden in on the others accumulating there. Reaching the back of Wetzel's place without being seen, Jim gestured the captives on into the building.

"Keep 'em snug and keep 'em quiet," he told Monk and Fronnie. "There's somebody else I want around for the powwow we've got shaping up. I'll be back directly."

He realized neither of his companions approved of this solitary foray, whatever its purpose, but he gave them back glare for glare and they reluctantly disappeared through Wetzel's back door with their captives.

Jim went on down the alley to the street at its other end. This also gave him a view into the plaza, and of the *palacio* at its far side. He was surprised to see that the old government building was entirely dark. The activity in the plaza certainly could not pass unnoticed in the governor's house. And in Charlie Bent's absence Carlita would be especially troubled by it.

In addition, she would have heard by now of the disappearance of Jim and his companions—perhaps even of the kidnaping of young Archuleta and Dolores Portola. She would not be sleeping with so much afoot in Santa Fe and Jim could not account for the dark windows. He wanted to investigate, but the search stirred by Fernando Portola was still continuing, in ignorance of the fact that the old man and his sons had themselves now also disappeared, and Jim did not dare risk crossing to the *palacio* and being cornered by the rifle-bearing New Mexicans centering their search in the square.

Keeping to shadow where he could, Jim cut around behind La Fonda, ducking into the recess of one of the old hotel's service doors to escape the notice of a party of men hurrying along toward the plaza. Twice more he encountered other ranging parties before he was clear of the old part of town and had started climbing the foothills toward the new section where Toni Palliard's house was. His luck was good, however, and he was not seen.

Jim paused once where he had a view back over the lower town. From here he had a curious impression belying his own knowledge. From here it seemed the

134

old city slept as it usually did, deeply and peacefully, after the fashion of all sleepers in the Southwest. There was no murmur of sound from the men ranging the streets. There was no mutter of Spanish anger at kidnaping, trouble-making Yankees on the faint up-slope drift of breeze. And nowhere—even in the plaza itself—did winking lights betray the movement a afoot there.

Jim thought this was strange. There was no doubting the men abroad in Santa Fe tonight were angry men—men who believed themselves justified in their anger. And they were not abroad in defiance of the law, but rather to bolster the law and flush out those who had wronged them and stolen the daughter of an honored house. As a result, there was no reason why they should muffle expression of their righteous fury or why they should slink about unlighted in the darkness like men on evil business.

A tremendous unease was pressing in on Jim. The guns in the plaza—this unnatural silence. These were portents and he recognized them as such. There had been others, too. But he kept them from his mind. Later—yes. But not now. Now was the time to assemble those he was determined to question. Now was the time to demand explanation. With full explanation a man would no longer be forced to function on hunches and portents. He would know what he faced. This was what Jim wanted.

Toni Palliard's house was as dark as the *palacio* had been. Jim climbed the path from the gate and knocked imperatively, but he received no response. He tried the shutters by which he had gained entry before. They were securely fastened from within. So were those on the other windows.

Apparently the young widow had learned from his first visit and had taken precautions to avoid any more unwanted callers. It was equally apparent she was not home. There was no other logical place in the city for her to be at this hour of the night. Jim was forced to fall back on a hunch again, in spite of his desire for certainty. This hunch, which he did not even try to justify to himself, was that Toni Palliard had gone to whatever destination Luis Sebastian and Juan Archuleta had been setting out for when they left Sebastian's house earlier in the evening.

Disappointed, but not daring to be gone too long from the group in Wetzel's cellar, Jim started back toward the center of town. He circled wide to avoid the plaza and so come up to the *palacio* from the rear. In the governor's absence, he thought it wise to have Carlita Bent present in the cellar when his hostages answered the questions he intended to put to them.

Nearing La Fonda, traveling a narrow street carefully selected for its emptiness, Jim heard a whisper of movement behind him. He wheeled. A man, coming up fast on moccasins as silent as his own, was almost on him. Jim jerked his pistol free and flipped the hammer back, but before he could fire the man skidded to a halt, calling out in alarm.

"Damn it, Jim—hold it!"

Jim lowered the gun in half anger, recognizing St. Vrain's voice. St. Vrain was half angry, too.

"What's the matter with you? Touchier than a sore-tailed bear. You like to nailed me!"

"Would have served you right for jumping me without any warning!"

"Jumping you?" St. Vrain grunted. "Why, I been

136

trailin you half a mile, tryin' to come up on you without bellowin' your name over half the town! What's been goin' on here, anyway? First I hear you're back. Then you've turned wagon-pirate an' got that popgun killer of a Tommie Defoe with you. Now I come in from Taos an' find you've disappeared—you an' Fronnie an' Monk an' Kincaid—an' you've swiped old man Portola's girl. The whole town looking for you with blood in its eye an' you wandering around the streets like you owned 'em! Can't I go off an' mind my business like I ought without you whopping up more trouble than ten men ought?"

Jim started to answer, then fell silent at the clatter of a recklessly ridden horse, hammering into town on the highroad from Glorietta Pass and the east. The horse passed at the next street corner, too distant for its rider to be recognized. But one thing was sure. The urgency of his errand was greater than his regard for the animal he rode or his own life, either one.

Realizing that St. Vrain and himself might at any minute attract the attention of the searchers still combing the town, Jim dragged his friend into the deeply arched gateway of a woodyard. Speaking swiftly, omitting detail, he recounted the situation which faced him on his return to Santa Fe from St. Louis, and what had developed since that time. He wound up with his present determination to see Carlita Bent and get her aid in forcing the truth of the situation in Santa Fe out of the prisoners he was holding in Wetzel's cellar.

St. Vrain shook his head with grave concern.

"Carlita isn't in Santa Fe, Jim," he said. "Charlie's still tied up in Taos and she's gone up there to be with him. Leal, the state's attorney, and most of the rest of Charlie's government has gone up with her."

"Most of the government—" Jim repeated. "Then that's it! That's what they've been waiting for—what they've been juggling for!"

"What is?"

"The best time to spring the scheme Sebastian's had all along—or Duval has had. And if the *palacio*'s empty of official government, then the best time in the world is right now! There'd sure be no point in waiting."

"Damn you, Jim, will you quit sputtering and try to make sense? Waiting for what?"

"A try at hauling a new flag up in front of the *palacio*!"

"You're crazy!" St. Vrain aid with conviction.

"It's the answer—it has to be!"

"You're goin' off like a gun barrel that's open at both ends," St. Vrain protested. "Sebastian and Duval are in business—in the business of trading merchandise, not in the business of setting off revolts. Where's the profit for them in getting mixed up in something like you're talking about?"

"How about an agreement beforehand that they'll get all the trade in and out of Santa Fe under the new government?"

St. Vrain shook his head slowly.

"Sebastian's nasty enough to do anything to throw a scare into competition. We all know that. But he ought to be smart enough to know politics is too big a job for him. The stakes are too high and the risk is too big. Duval, now—he's a horse of a different color. He's got the money and he's got the power, and he thinks big enough for something like that. But he's not in Santa Fe, and nobody could run a rebellion here from outside. Sebastian is just kickin' up a dust cloud to force everybody out of the local trade if he can. That's all this is. It's got to be."

"Come on back to Wetzel's with me," Jim urged. "I'll make some of those boys shell out with the truth. Then maybe you'll believe me!"

"Maybe," St. Vrain agreed thoughtfully.

CHAPTER 14

STORM

JIM AND ST. VRAIN MADE THEIR WAY CAREFULLY down the street. Jim was impatient and angry with his companion. Ceran St. Vrain was widely respected, first as a business man and a trader, and then as one of the wisest of the mountain men. But he was being blind now. Stubborn, mule blindness, too. The whole picture was clearing so rapidly for Jim, he knew he could make the governor's partner see it, if St. Vrain would only open his eyes. And St. Vrain was important—terribly important.

There were a few regular soldiers under Colonel Price at the Santa Fe garrison cantonment, a few miles out from the plaza. Just about a big enough force to make a creditable military appearance at a changing of the colors, and that was all. There had been enough men armed with new trade rifles in the plaza tonight to overrun Colonel Price's little command in one charge.

The best hope for order lay in the militia, largely composed of men from the States, and nominally under St. Vrain's command. Of course, Santa Fe was actually a base for roaming Yankees, rather than a permanent residence, and few of the enrollment were in the city at any given time. And Ceran, in the easy scorn of the lone

139

hunter for military maneuver, had never drilled his men. He probably could not scare up more than thirty rifles in Santa Fe tonight. But thirty were better than none. And if good men were behind the sights, disaster might be avoided.

Jim cursed the complacency of officialdom. General Kearney had taken the rest of his army on to California. It would take him weeks to make the difficult return march and it was doubtful Washington would order him to do so. Aside from a small bloc in Congress, headed by Senator Benton, the national government regarded New Mexico as an arid waste which had already cost too much money, time, and powder. It seemed likely that if revolt did flare and was successful, the Territory would be abandoned by the rest of the country. At least long enough for a clever trader to rake together an immense fortune from even a brief monopoly of the trade.

Ceran was right in one thing. It was too big thinking for Luis Sebastian. Jim remembered Edouard Duval's offers of profit to himself and his bland threats the night he and Tommie Defoe had faced the trader. He wondered if Duval was still in St. Louis. He wondered if Sebastian was actually still alone in Santa Fe.

His reflections were broken at the next corner, where a few minutes before the reckless rider had flashed across the street he and St. Vrain were following, coming in on the highroad from Glorietta Pass and the east. There was more traffic at the corner.

Heads low from a long night drive, six-span teams were dragging one heavy freight wagon after another past the crossing. Jim recognized the shape of the crates loading the first three wagons. They were trade rifle containers, twelve guns to the case.

140

Three men rode behind the third wagon. One was Juan Archuleta who had ridden from Sebastian's house with him soon after sunset. The second was Sebastian, himself. The third was the man whom Sebastian and Archuleta had ridden out to meet as he came in off of the interminable trail from the river. There could be no mistaking the great, grotesque body of Edouard Duval.

Jim looked at St. Vrain. The mountain man's usually genial features were set in an iron mask.

"Get back to Wetzel's," he whispered. "Twist arms. Pull fingernails out by the roots. Bust bones—bust heads. But find out plans and details—fast! And when! That's what we've got to know for sure. Use the people you've got for hostages, if you can. Anything to give us a little time. I'll warn Colonel Price and round up all the men I can. But we're in real trouble, Jim. All New Mexico is!"

"Santa Fe's enough to worry about tonight, far as I'm concerned," Jim said.

"I thought you was a bright boy," St. Vrain said. "It's worse than that. You told me everybody in town was armed tonight. Look how many more guns they're bringing in on those wagons. And the supply wagon was carrying enough duffel for a lot bigger string of freight. I'd guess a good part of the train was already split off and headed north."

"Toward the pueblos—then they're arming the Indians!"

"I'd say they intend to try."

"Then we can't stop them."

"Maybe not. But the least we can do is try, too. I'll get the best man I can find off to warn Charlie at Taos. But it's up to us to hold Santa Fe for him somehow. If we lose the plaza, we've lost the Territory."

141

Jim nodded. They separated. The shadows swallowed St. Vrain without a sound. Jim swung into an easy, swift, silent Indian lope toward Wetzel's store. The cry of *"caravaneros"* was sweeping the heretofore silent town—Santa Fe's traditional welcome to freighters. But there was a new timbre to it—a more clarion note than the usual excitement over new merchandise fresh in from the States. Jim could hear it plainly in the shouts marking the progress of the wagons toward the private corral behind the Duval & Co. store.

The excitement made his own passage easier. It almost wholly absorbed the interest of those who had been searching for him. If a vestige of doubt remained over the conviction he had expressed to St. Vrain, it evaporated now. The sound and the taste and the electric vibration of rebellion were in the air.

Luck was with him and he made it safely to Wetzel's doorway. He was immediately startled, however, by the condition of the little trader's store. For a moment he was afraid the hiding place of his comrades and their prisoners had been discovered. Then he realized the disarray and destruction was the work of vandals who had taken advantage of the broken locks on the front door—or had heard of Sebastian's mistreatment of Wetzel and had concluded there was no one in Santa Fe now to protect his interests.

Jim kicked through the debris to the trap door and raised it cautiously.

Candles, snuffed at the sound of his approach, were relighted. Kincaid, with his bandaged leg stretched out on a cask before him, was efficiently sitting guard over a sullen group composed of the Portola men, young Archuleta, Henry Chavez, and the unidentified man Jim and his companions had trapped at the end of the alley.

This group did not share Fronnie's relief at Jim's reappearance. They stared stolidly—challengingly—at him.

Near them, but a little apart, sat Tommie Defoe. Dolores Portola was beside him. Jim sensed that this juxtaposition was Tommie's choice, rather than the girl's. She was white-faced, tense, weary with strain, and she paid no attention to the man beside her. She kept her glance consciously averted from her father and her brothers, but it was apparent that her frightened attention was wholly engrossed in them.

Defoe's features were bland as always. He showed neither displeasure nor relief at Jim's appearance. He seemed to have reverted wholly to the sardonic man Jim had met in St. Louis. When Jim's glance crossed his, Defoe smiled slightly, as though with some small, secret amusement. Jim matched the smile. Among those who would talk presently was Defoe.

The most startling presence in the cellar was another woman, kneeling beside Saul Wetzel, skillfully pulling tight bindings around the injured trader's chest, using strips torn from a near-by bolt of trade cloth. Wetzel had regained consciousness, and in spite of the tugging, he was already obviously more comfortable. He looked up at Jim, but his glance returned immediately to the girl who was bandaging him. Jim crossed to stand above her. She raised her head slowly.

"I am glad you are back, Jim," she said.

"How the hell did you get here?"

Toni Palliard returned to her bandaging of Wetzel's chest without answer. Fronnie, shaking his head resentfully, appeared at Jim's elbow.

"You'd a thought she come out of a rifled gun!" Fronnie said. "And pointed right at us. Come ridin' like

143

an Apache up the alley an' started hammerin' on the back door, screamin' for Saul like she had a message from the devil hisself!"

Kincaid grinned.

" 'S a fact, Jim," he corroborated. "An' ol' Fronnie reckoned he'd go shut her up a fore she brung the whole town in on us. Good man, Fronnie. Didn't lose no more'n half his face hide, doin' it—an' then had to bring her back down here 'cause she wouldn't have it any other way."

Jim saw, then, the nail marks raw across one of Fronnie's cheeks.

"Ain't polite to hit a woman or it'd been different," Fronnie growled.

Toni Palliard rose to face Jim.

"I would have hunted for you, Jim, but I didn't know where you were or how to find you. And I had to have somebody who would realize the importance of what I had to tell them. I tried the *palacio*, but Mrs. Bent was gone. I didn't know where to turn , Mr. Wetzel was the only one I could think of."

"There was always me, Toni," Defoe said quietly.

The young widow flashed Tommie an edged look of accusation and scorn. He shrugged easily.

"All right," he said. "It's the same old story. You always try to do things the wrong way. You'd better leave this to me. You'll regret it if you don't."

"Shut up, Tommie," Jim snapped. "You'll get your turn later."

Defoe shrugged again, apparently undisturbed, and Jim turned back to Toni Palliard.

"Tonight's the first time Saul or myself have been hard to find. Why wait so long?"

"Because only tonight did I really understand what

144

was going to happen. Jim, Mr. Duval is in Santa Fe."

"I know," Jim said. "I've seen him."

"But you don't know why he's here. I didn't either until I learned Sebastian was riding out to meet him and so rode out into the pass myself. Duval has financed a revolt in Santa Fe, and Luis has it all planned."

Tommie Defoe lost his half smile. He leaned forward, a powerful urgency in the softness of his voice.

"Toni, I warned you!"

"Do you think you count now?" the girl asked. "Do you think you ever did really?"

"You spoiled a fine plan for me once, Toni," Defoe said, his voice growing even more soft. "I'll not let you do it again."

Frontenac glanced at Jim, then eased over and sat down in comradely fashion beside Defoe, dropping a great hand onto the little man's knee.

"Jim told you to shut up," he advised pleasantly. "You'd better do it. He don't like repeating himself."

Defoe looked at the big mountain man and showed his teeth without a smile. But he quieted.

"Go on," Jim said to Toni Palliard.

"Luis Sebastian has some kind of an agreement with Señor Portola, there. Luis has issued guns. When the revolt strikes, Duval and Luis get the Santa Fe trade. Señor Portola and his friends get a new government of their own. And the Yankees of Santa Fe get a bullet in the head—all of them."

"Guesses," Tommie Defoe said. "Believe me, Jim. Like I've been guessing. She isn't in on this, any more than I am. Both of us have had our own schemes. But not this."

"Is she right?"

Defoe hunched his shoulders.

145

"Just what difference does that make now? There's nothing you can do in any case, Jim. There's nothing any of your friends can do. I warned you out of Santa Fe and so did Toni. Why didn't you go?"

"Why the warning, if you didn't know what was coming?" Jim asked the girl.

Defoe rose to his feet.

"You were in her way, Jim—or she was afraid you would be. There's a nasty story about Duval and Toni's mother. She hasn't had a warm drop of blood in her veins because of revenge. She came here and waited for Duval to get here, too—waited until his plans had gone so far he couldn't back out and she was sure she could destroy him. That's what she's trying now. And using you for executioner."

"That's not true, Tommie!" Toni Palliard protested.

"Close enough," Defoe said. "But you gambled wrong, Toni. You're going now by who you want to win, not by who is going to. Duval's got the whole Territory in his pocket, thanks to Sebastian and Señor Portola and his friends. Don't bank on Jim here, or you'll lose—just like you, Jim, if you don't get out of here in a hurry.

Defoe turned back to Toni Palliard and gripped her arm.

"The cards are all stacked for us, Toni," he said. "They don't fall this way very often. Keep out of this and keep Duval thinking you've been with him from the beginning. When the smoke's cleared out of this miserable collection of mud huts, we won't have helped anything happen that wouldn't have happened anyway, and we'll have money!"

"We!" the girl cried. "I didn't come to Santa Fe for you—or for money!"

She gripped Jim's arm.

"I don't know how much time is left, but I'm afraid there isn't much. You've got to warn all the Yankees in Santa Fe before they're murdered in their beds!"

Jim strode across to Fernando Portola.

"Is this true?"

The old man snorted.

"Believe the woman if you will," he said. "Believe her words to be truth. But even if they are, what good is truth when you only have the half of it, Señor? How can you warn your countrymen when you do not know when the blow will fall? Besides, you are not a people who keep track of one another. How would you find them all? Take Señor Defoe's advice. Free us and get out of Santa Fe while you can. We will permit it if you act now."

Jim's anger rose sharply at the blandness of the old man's offer of personal amnesty. But there was something else—the threat that all Yankees would be killed. He had not thought of this and neither had St. Vrain. Both had swiftly thought of recruits—of riflemen—the thin force of fighting men which might be raised to defend the city. But they had not considered the women and children.

"You will be the first to die," he told Portola.

The old man looked at him with a devastating scorn.

"This is a threat? Señor, not even God himself knows how many Portolas have died for Spain and for Mexico. It is well that a few of us die for New Mexico, too. Do what you will. It will change nothing."

Jim looked over his prisoners, wondering which would be the most likely to break when pressure of physical agony was put against them. There seemed no other way.

Perhaps his reluctance was in his eyes, or it was obvious he had no other choice. The men grew uncomfortable without an easing of their dark-eyed defiance. After an interminable moment, Dolores Portola drew a deep breath and rose to face her father and her brothers.

"I have not spoken to you before of what you do."

"A woman does not speak of such things!" the old man snapped.

"Nevertheless, I speak," the girl said steadily. "And you will hear me!"

"Jaime King is an honorable man," Dolores Portola began. "I know. You will believe me or I will tell you the reason I know, and let the honor of our house suffer."

Old Man Portola looked at his daughter for a long moment, then nodded curtly.

"We will agree. Jaime King is an honorable man. I know of none who would say otherwise."

"Then, Father, he is a good *yanqui*. If there is one good *yanqui,* there must be others. And if there are good *yanquis,* there are bad ones. This is also true?"

"We will agree—it is true."

"You do the wrong, then. You deal with the bad ones. What they have planned here will bring hurt to us all and gain us nothing but shame. Our family is my family, too. I have the right to say my say in a family matter."

"This is no family matter and you have no right!" Feliz Portola growled.

"I speak to you, Father," Dolores implored the old man. "You have made it your business to know where all of the *yanquis* in Santa Fe may be found. All of the ones who have been marked for death. Let them be warned."

148

The old man glared at the girl for a long moment without speaking, his lips thinning to a straight line.

"To this we do not agree!" he said.

The girl's shoulders fell. She turned to Frontenac and pointed to her father.

"In his pocket is a chart and a list of the places they are to be found," she said.

Fronnie started forward. The group of New Mexicans tensed. Kincaid and Mooney covered them with eagerly ready guns. Old Portola brushed Fronnie's demanding hand away and with great dignity surrendered a sheaf of papers from his pockets.

"I am too old a man to let any woman—even a trusted daughter of my own blood—know all of an important plan. If I had been so foolish, this one here would already know what you now try to find out—"

He pointed to Defoe.

"He has tempted my daughter as best he could to win this end. But he failed—and so shall you, Señor King. You have the list, but when any of you leave here to carry your warning, you risk discovery of where you hide—where you hide us. I beg of you to go now, and take that risk. I beg you to attempt warning the town. To what end can you do so? You can warn of death, of course. But when will this death strike? Can your people be on guard at all doors, twenty-four hours a day? Will they even believe you when you are unable to say what the hour will be? Until you know this, you can do nothing to stop us, and this one answer you will not get, for I alone of those here know it!"

Looking at the haughty old man, Jim knew he spoke the truth. Even the Comanches knew no deviltry capable of making such a man talk against his will. So there still remained only a hunch upon which to go, and how did a

149

man guess the hour of another's whim?

"You are a brave man, Señor Portola," Jim said quietly. "I would respect you now if I had not before. But we already know."

Jim saw a flicker of doubt in the old eyes facing him. He massed all the assurance he could.

"The attack comes this morning—with the sun."

Archuleta, the young Portolas, and even Chavez paled, looking sharply to the old man. Fernando Portola held rigid and firm for a long moment, but the strain was too great. His shoulders sagged.

Tommie Defoe, who had been watching the old man alertly, turned to Jim with wry humor dancing in his eyes.

"Looks like I've backed the wrong game again," he said. "Start giving orders, Jim. I can't play against blind luck. I may be a fool, but I've been one before. Maybe you've got a chance after all. I'll play along with you."

He stretched out his hand to Frontenac.

"Give me those lists. I'll get the word around."

Jim looked at Defoe with strong distaste and shook his head.

"You'd make a hell of a grandmother, Jim," Tommie Defoe said. "Do you want to stop this thing or not?"

"We can do it without you, Defoe."

"How?" Tommie countered "You and your friends don't dare leave this cellar. You'd be discovered before you got to the next corner. Your whole advantage would be lost before you could do a damned thing. But I can move freely. Sebastian thinks I'm with him—or at least hopes I am."

"There isn't any other way, Jaime King," the Portola girl said. "I'll go with Señor Defoe."

"So will I," Toni Palliard added. "We'll divide those

lists between us."

Jim shook his head again.

"I don't trust you any more than I do Defoe."

"You should, Jim," Defoe said quietly. "Her interests are yours. Toni's planned a long time to break Duval's back. She won't let anything interfere with that now."

Jim looked at Frontenac and Kincaid and Mooney. They were scowling in dark disapproval.

"No good, Jim," Mooney said. "Pretty plain they've knowed each other a long time. Look like the same breed to me."

Fronnie and Kincaid nodded agreement.

"You've known Toni quite a while yourself, Jim," Defoe went on. "Longer than you think. One night she took a warning shot at me at Duval's house in St. Louis because she was afraid we'd upset her plans for the man who killed her mother and broke her father's heart."

Jim stiffened. His eyes turned slowly to the young widow. He remembered her as he had seen her in her own house here, gowned for bed. And he remembered also the hooded dancer he had seen at the Fontaine and again in Duval's house. He had seen the face of only one, but he had seen the bodies of both, and he should have known that two such figures could not exist in the world. In this identification, at least, Defoe was telling the truth.

"Toni and I grew up on the same street in New Orleans," Tommie went on. "In happier days I suppose we were sweethearts, like kids are. But that was a long time ago. Her name is not Palliard nor La Fleur, but Toni Bandelier. She might have had me, but I liked money too much—I always have. And I've wanted her to take her revenge out of Duval's moneybags. That wasn't enough for her."

151

"Maybe it was more that you just weren't enough of a man, Tommie," the girl said quietly.

"That, too—freely admitted," Defoe said. "Don't believe me, Jim. I'd lie to you now, if I could see gold in it. But believe her. She's never had a husband. She's never been 'Mrs.' anybody. And I think she's the bravest person I've ever known—the most honest. She's had to use her own weapons, but she fights fairer than any man."

"Well, Jim King?" the girl asked.

Jim nodded slowly.

"Go ahead—the three of you. Send everybody you can out to the military encampment. They'll be safe there. The men who are armed can join Colonel Price and Ceran St. Vrain. We'll see."

"What will you do here?" Toni Bandelier asked.

"Wait for the sun—or for Señor Portola and his friends to come to their senses and call this off."

"And afterward?"

"We'll wait for the sun and see."

CHAPTER 15

SUNRISE

THERE WAS UTTER SILENCE IN THE CELLAR FOR several minutes after Defoe and the two girls climbed the ladder and vanished through the trap. The New Mexicans made a tight little group about Fernando Portola. Fronnie and Kincaid and Mooney drew apart and whispered among themselves in soundless council. Jim sank wearily down beside Wetzel and discovered the trader's eyes on him in speculation.

152

"It's not as bad as it seems," Jim said quietly, keeping his voice too low to be audible to Portola's group. "I bumped into St. Vrain. He's gone to Price and sent word north to Taos. He and the Colonel will be in from the army camp soon with what men they can raise."

"If we had every man in the Territory here, we'd be outnumbered," Wetzel said.

"I know," Jim agreed. "And they sent several wagons loaded with guns up the valley."

"Toward the pueblos?"

Jim nodded.

"The Indians, then. If they come down on us, too—"

Jim nodded again. Wetzel closed his eyes. Fronnie stood up and came over to where Jim sat.

"Been a time or two you've listened to us, Jim," he began.

"I'm listening, Fronnie."

"We've got Papa Portola and these other back-stabbers. They got friends outside that ain't going to want to see them die. Put a pistol to their heads and let's get out of here. Let's get up where we can see the sunrise. If the rest know we mean business with these, maybe they'll back off."

"If they don't?"

"Shoot the lot of 'em that we've got, like the dogs they are, and try to carve our way through the rest. We might make it. You an' Monk an' Kincaid an' me have done pretty good before when we was boxed in tight."

"Not this time, Fronnie," Jim said. "Maybe, if Portola's friends were the only ones involved. But Duval and Sebastian won't stop at anything, once this starts. They don't dare. They'd let Portola and these others die without turning a hair. They've got more than blood and country and resentment wrapped up in this—

153

they've got more than any New Mexican. There's millions in profit to be had, and that's what they're after."

Fronnie's shoulders drooped dispiritedly. Jim looked at the heavy floor beams overhead and the dank cobblestoned walls of the cellar. Suddenly he too was physically oppressed and longed for the smell of outer air.

"How long since Defoe and the women left?" he said, after a while.

"A bit short of an hour, I'd reckon," Wetzel answered.

"We can't wait any longer," Jim said, raising his voice. "Be daylight any time. Let's go up."

There was no comment. Fronnie helped Wetzel to his feet and supported him toward the ladder. Mooney helped Kincaid. Fernando Portola and his sons and their friends filed quietly ahead of Jim. The whole group knotted in Wetzel's sleeping quarters in the trade room above. Jim pulled back one of the partitioning curtains. Gray light perceptibly brightened the plaza beyond the front windows. He turned back to his prisoners and faced Fernando Portola.

"I don't expect you to stand against your own people," he said quietly. "I don't expect you to try stopping them when they discover us. But I do expect you to keep quiet and out of the way."

Fernando Portola shook his head.

"No promises," he said.

Jim shrugged.

"The first one of you to make a sound or otherwise attract attention will be shot," he said.

He stepped through the partitioning curtains and slipped along to the front windows. Light was growing

154

in the plaza. The New Mexicans who had been searching for Jim and his companions with varying diligence through the night were now gathering in groups in the square, quietly waiting. An ominous quiet seemed to have descended on the old town. There was no sign of Sebastian and Duval and their personal men. Nor was there any indication that Defoe and the girls had reached any of the city's Yankees, or that St. Vrain had reached Colonel Price's tiny command. Jim moved back to Wetzel's quarters.

Fernando Portola had lit a cigar and was sitting on the foot of Wetzel's bed, where Wetzel was now propped. The trader moved his feet a little farther aside and Jim sat down beside Portola.

"I'd give you good advice, if you'd listen," he told the old man.

Portola looked blankly at him.

"I think as much of this old town as you do," Jim went on. "I used to think I had good friends here— friends as fair to me as I tried to be to them in my trading."

The blankness of Portola's answering stare did not change.

"I can't believe a man as wise as you won't see the truth," Jim continued. "This revolt you've planned isn't for freedom or better government. It's for Duval and Sebastian. And they'll be the first to turn against you when Washington sends troops out to support Colonel Price and Governor Bent."

"Washington will be supporting dead men," Feliz Portola snapped.

"Maybe so," Jim conceded, "But when the troops do get here, your mother will see the hanging of her husband and her sons."

The old man sucked on his cigar and said nothing. Jim rose and went back out through the blankets to the plaza windows again. Kincaid hobbled up beside him. They stared wordlessly out onto the square. The waiting groups were growing larger. Their attention seemed chiefly on the *palacio* across the plaza. Jim guessed this would be their first objective when vioelence flared. It was a symbol of the government they sought to overthrow. It had been such a symbol many times before. And when they had taken the old building , then would come the wholesale extermination of what Yankees could be found in the town. After that—it depended upon how many of the Indians had been armed, how much of the Territory beyond the city had been included in the plot Duval and Sebastian had so successfully encouraged.

Kincaid scrubbed his chin with one hand.

"We're sure goin' to a lot of trouble to get you back into business!" he murmured.

"Seems like," Jim agreed. "Be great to be off somewhere in the mountains on a trapline and out of this, wouldn't it?"

Kincaid colored a bit at the dryness of Jim's tone.

"I didn't say that!" he protested.

Frontenac joined them and eyed the plaza.

"Gettin' bright enough for good shootin' light out there," he said. "Defoe an' them women could have lit straight out for the hills and saved their own bacon."

"Yeah, or run straight to Sebastian with news of where we are and how we're fixed,'' Jim added.

Fronnie's eyes rounded at this thought. He started to say something else, but he was interrupted by a stir in the plaza. Diagonally across, where the largest group of rebels was assembled, four men made their appearance.

156

They were Juan Archuleta, George Mohler, Sebastian, and Edouard Duval. They conferred a moment with members of the group, then led off along the walk toward the old *palacio*. The rest surged forward, cheering loudly, and following.

Suddenly, from the opposite side of the plaza, a shot sounded—the thin, high snap of a heavily charged, small caliber rifle. Duval instantly reeled, throwing one arm up against the side of his grotesque head. Sebastian and Mohler tried to catch him, but he was a dead weight and his body slipped from their grasp to the walk. A cry went up from the rebels, and the various groups melded together, charging angrily toward the sound of the shot.

"Defoe!" Fronnie bellowed in delayed recognition. "Know that gun anywhere!"

He lunged past Jim and out on the walk. Mooney, loping across the store, boiled outside a bare yard behind Fronnie. They fired and drew instant response. Sebastian swung with a part of the rebels toward the front of Wetzel's store. Jim shouldered onto the walk, also, with Kincaid behind him. They fanned out beside Mooney and Frontenac, their guns joining the dawn thunder.

Sebastian instantly lost his enthusiasm for leadership and fell back among his followers. Jim was a moment in realizing the man was being driven back—not by cowardice—but by the impact of bullets tearing into his body, and that the four of them on the walk before Wetzel's were all firing at the same target. Torn and reeling, Sebastian's body was held up by the press of men about it for just a moment. Then it fell and disappeared.

A yell sounded beyond the *palacio*—the wild, high rendezvous yell of mountain men—and a new group poured into the plaza. Uniforms were visible, and suits of fringed buckskin. Ceran St. Vrain, joyously playing at soldier and being a commander, marched at the head of the group, beside Colonel Price.

From the side from which the first shot had come, another group appeared. Tommie Defoe was not among them, but they comprised every loyal man in Santa Fe not already found by St. Vrain, and it was with a great surge of pleasure that Jim saw many native New Mexicans among them.

Caught in the middle between these two forces, and discovering themselves suddenly without leadership, the rebels in the plaza began throwing down their arms. Jim and Mooney and Frontenac ran recklessly out into the square, rifles high and horizontal in a truce signal, and the firing came to an end.

Jim's prisoners emerged from Wetzel's store. St. Vrain, broadly flourishing an officer's sword he'd found time to borrow somewhere, rushed up with some troopers behind him, and signaled the soldiers to take the New Mexicans off. St. Vrain turned on Jim then, glowering.

"Trying to do the whole job yourself?" he accused.

"It's what you get for stopping to eat breakfast on the way," Jim told him. "What about the pueblos—the Indians?"

"Peaceable and quiet," St. Vrain said with considerable self-satisfaction. "That's what delayed me and the colonel. We caught up with Duval's other wagons afore they was five miles out of town."

"Seen Defoe?"

St. Vrain shook his head. A passing man heard the query. He stopped and pointed off across the town.

"He was down by the Duval and Company store a

couple minutes ago."

Jim turned to Colonel Price who was just coming up.

"Sebastian and Duval are both dead and their hands probably scattering for timber as fast as they can go. There's cash assets in Duval's store to be protected until somebody figures out who they be belong to."

The officer nodded and trotted purposefully off, assembling a detail of his men as he moved. Jim saw Toni Bandelier and Dolores Portola pushing through the crowd. He rescued them and brought them up to St. Vrain.

"Here's the two to whom we owe the most, Ceran," he said.

He made introductions. St. Vrain acknowledged them in his most courtly manner. Jim saw the sparkle of appreciation in the mountain man's eye and moved quickly in beside Toni Bandelier.

"Set your own traps!" he warned St. Vrain.

"You and Charlie Bent!" St. Vrain complained. "Charlie goes off to Taos and leaves me all this to get straightened out. And then, by hell, while my back's turned you grab the prettiest girl in sight!"

Jim grinned, then sobered when he saw the sadness in Dolores Portola's eyes.

"The Colonel, here, has a lot of influence with Governor Bent, Señorita," he said. "If we asked him nice, I've got a hunch he'd go along with you and help pry your father and your brothers away from the soldiers who took them off."

"Now, wait a minute, Jim—" St. Vrain protested. "That ain't legal!"

"You're taking Charlie's place. You said so yourself. And you know how Charlie is. He wouldn't want his most influential citizens in jail. Since they didn't actually fight against us, I doubt he'd want to hold them."

St. Vrain looked at the Portola girl and became courtly all over again. He winked at Jim.

"Bless you, partner," he said. "I should have known you'd save old Ceran something good. Come along, Señorita, and we'll have a talk with those soldiers. If Charlie don't like it when he gets back, he can take it up with me."

Dolores, radiant with relief and not at all displeased with the attentions of so important a man as Ceran St. Vrain, tucked her arm in his and they moved off.

Jim found himself alone in Wetzel's doorway with Toni.

"Bandelier—" he said.

She nodded.

"No husband—"

"And no means of support," she agreed.

"I'll make a deal to remedy that," a voice wheezed behind them.

They turned. Saul Wetzel leaned against a counter within the store, favoring his painful ribs but smiling at the girl.

"What kind of a deal, Saul?" Jim asked.

Before the trader could answer, there was a commotion on the walk, and Jim's name was called. Colonel Price located him and came briskly up.

"The Duval store cash drawer was broken into, King. Broken into and emptied. By one man, carrying a light rifle. Stole a saddle and a horse from the corral, too, the hostler down there says. Helped himself to blankets and trail kit and grub from the stock. Can't have much of a start. Think we can spare a detail to go after him?"

Jim shook his head. Price turned to a junior officer.

"Let him go. We're too short-handed to spare a detachment now."

The soldiers moved off. Price followed them. Toni touched Jim's arm.

"Tommie?" she asked.

"If he collected a few wages, I guess he's earned them," Jim said with a nod.

He turned back to Wetzel.

"You were offering a deal, Saul," he reminded the trader.

"With the little lady," Wetzel agreed. "You talk Jim into forgetting the rest of what I owe him on that contraband freight I took off his hands, and going into a partnership with me, and I'll see he gives you a job waiting trade."

Toni looked at Jim. Jim in turn looked out into the plaza where townsmen, subdued by the sound of guns and the stain of fresh blood in the dust of Santa Fe, were helping Price and his men carry away the bodies of those who had fallen with Sebastian and Edouard Duval. Those who were not occupied were waiting, uncertain as to what might come next. What all Santa Fe needed now was partnership—partnership of the old and the new. On this basis she could grow.

As for himself, it was always said among the mountian legion that a partner had to be a man to ride the river with. Saul Wetzel had proved himself to be such a man.

"Tell Mr. Wetzel we'll take his deal," he told Toni.

And in the back of his mind there was a new hope—a sly little hope—that Carlita Bent was not a jealous woman. From now on, the governor's wife would not be the uncontested queen of the mountain men. Not when men of the legion spoke also of Jim King's woman.

We hope that you enjoyed reading this
Sagebrush Large Print Western.
If you would like to read more Sagebrush titles,
ask your librarian or contact the Publishers:

United States and Canada

Thomas T. Beeler, *Publisher*
Post Office Box 659
Hampton Falls, New Hampshire 03844-0659
(800) 251-8726

United Kingdom, Eire, and
the Republic of South Africa

Isis Publishing Ltd
7 Centremead
Osney Mead
Oxford OX2 0ES England
(01865) 250333

Australia and New Zealand

Australian Large Print Audio & Video P/L
17 Mohr Street
Tullamarine, Victoria, 3043, Australia
1 800 335 364